THE UNKNOWNS
A MYSTERY

THE UNK

BENEDICT CAREY

AMULET BOOKS
NEW YORK

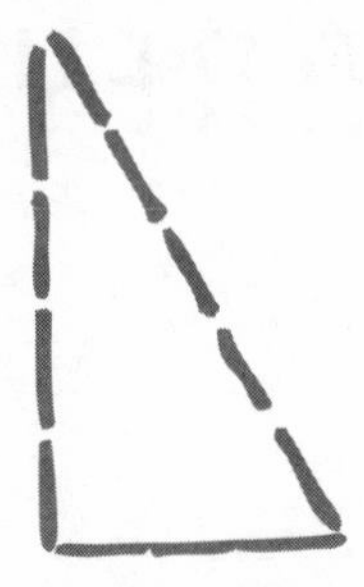

PUBLISHER'S NOTE: This is a work of fiction. Names, characters, places, and incidents are either the product of the author's imagination or are used fictitiously, and any resemblance to actual persons, living or dead, business establishments, events, or locales is entirely coincidental.

Library of Congress Cataloging-in-Publication Data

Carey, Benedict.
The unknowns / by Benedict Carey.
p. cm.
Summary: When people start vanishing from a godforsaken trailer park next to the Folsom Energy Plant, two eleven-year-olds investigate using mathematical clues that were hastily planted by their friend Mrs. Clarke before she disappeared.
ISBN 978-0-8109-7991-8
[1. Missing persons—Fiction. 2. Conspiracies—Fiction. 3. Mathematics—Fiction. 4. Trailer camps—Fiction. 5. Mystery and detective stories.] I. Title.

PZ7.C2122Un 2009
[Fic]—dc22
2008033914

Book design and interior illustrations by Chad W. Beckerman

Printed and bound in U.S.A.
10 9 8 7 6 5 4 3 2

ABRAMS
THE ART OF BOOKS SINCE 1949

115 West 18th Street
New York, NY 10011
www.abramsbooks.com

FOR VICTORIA,
ISABEL, AND FLORA

SPECIAL THANKS TO
KRISTINE DAHL,
AMALIA ELLISON,
SUSAN VAN METRE,
ERIKA ERHART,
AND JOHN HASTINGS.
AND TO THAYLENE BARRETT,
WAYNE BARRETT, AND JOHN DONICH
FOR CHECKING THE MATH. AND,
OF COURSE, TO THE CAREYS:
CATHERINE, JAMES,
RACHEL, SIMON,
AND NOAH

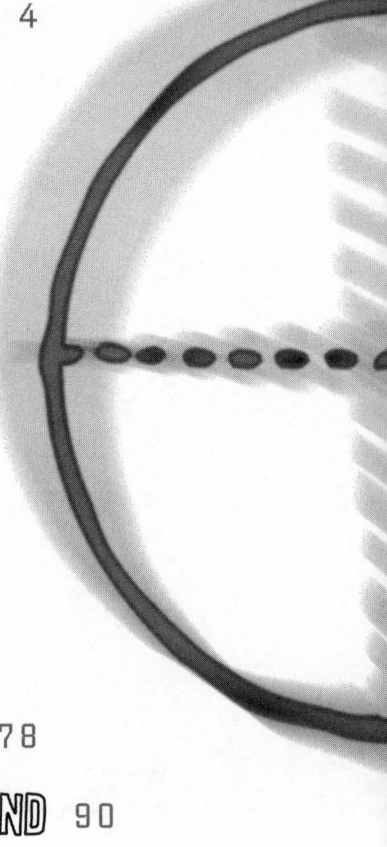

THE MAP

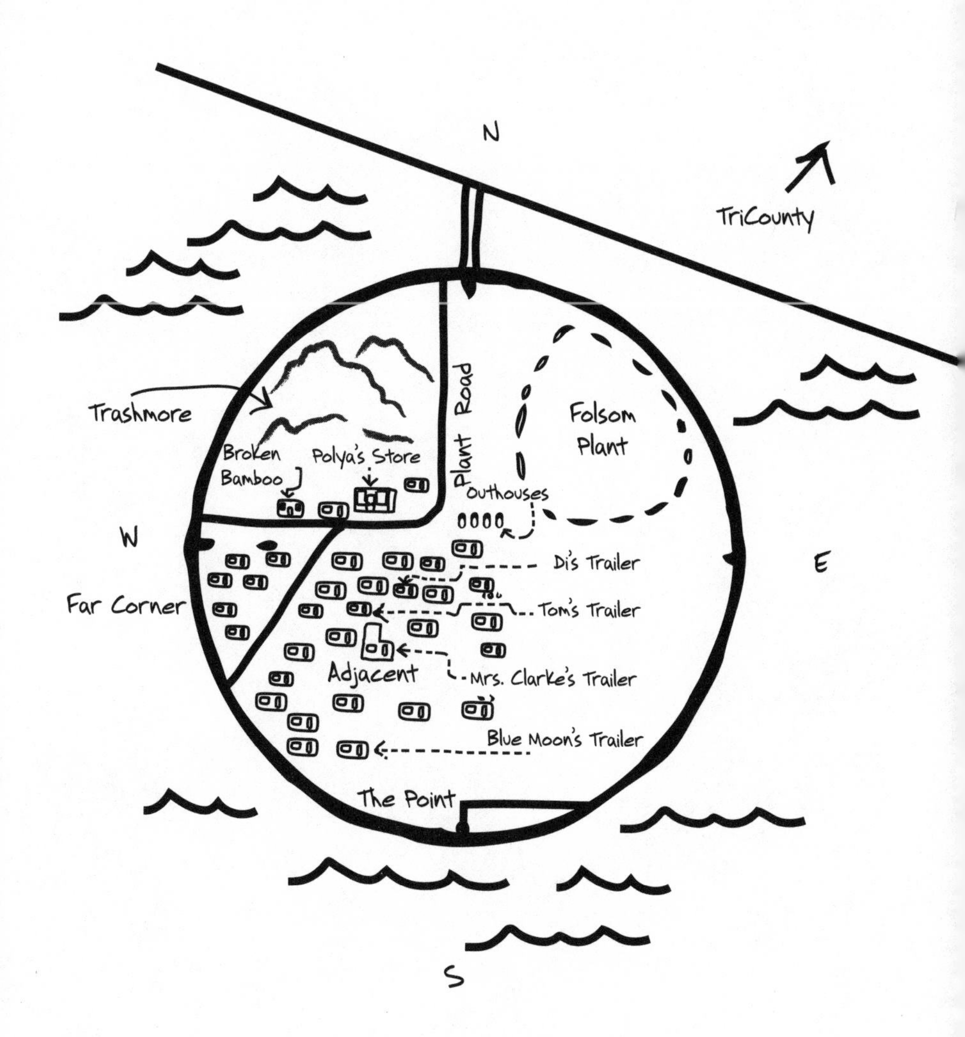
N
TriCounty
Trashmore
Plant Road
Folsom Plant
Broken Bamboo
Polya's Store
Outhouses
W
E
Di's Trailer
Far Corner
Tom's Trailer
Adjacent
Mrs. Clarke's Trailer
Blue Moon's Trailer
The Point
S

FOLSOM ADJACENT

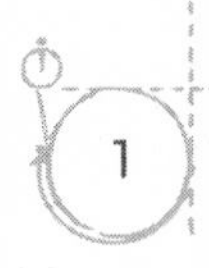

SO HERE'S THE THING, AND YOU CAN ASK ANYONE ABOUT it: People were praying for something twisted to happen last summer. They didn't care what it was, either. A hurricane, an earthquake, a hostage situation—seriously, anything. We wanted a problem, and a hairy one, just for something to do.

You would've too, if you lived where we did. Folsom Adjacent, it's called. Adjacent—*uh-JAY-sent*, is how you say it—means nearby or next to, so it doesn't even have its own name. Doesn't deserve it, really, because it's not much of a town, or a place. Or even a neighborhood.

Adjacent is a trailer park named after a nuclear plant, is what it is. Think of hundreds of beat-up mobile homes scattered around a gas station, a musty grocery store, a bar, and a desperate little elementary school, which was just two old trailers pushed together with a sign that said ADJACENT ELEMENTRY. Someone forgot the "a" and it never got fixed.

Adjacent is on a small island, a coastal island, close to shore. On a clear day you can see miniature people having normal lives over in the city across the way, Crotona. Crotona is too full of very important people for its own good but at least it's a real place, with actual stuff to do and see.

Adjacent's got nothing, no mall or multiplex or skate park. Even Folsom Energy, the giant plant where half the parents work, doesn't seem real. It was built entirely underground. All you see is a flat, dusty nothing surrounded by barbed wire and signs that say AUTHORIZED PERSONNEL ONLY all over the place. As if people wanted to sneak into that place. As if we weren't already trapped behind barbed wire, a million miles from anything, in a place where nothing ever happened.

Until one week in July, that is. That's when suddenly it looked like the praying might have worked: People in Adjacent began to disappear.

First there was Mickey Romo, some guy no one knew who lived alone in a trailer full of old computers. People said he liked to go out exploring at night, that he once scaled the cliffs down to the ocean. That he knew of caves down near the plant. Lunatic stuff. We thought, OK, so maybe this was just some loner who moved away, or got abducted by aliens or something.

But that didn't explain Mrs. Quartez. Mrs. Quartez was this

lady who worked nights at Folsom and used to play cards with her friends out in front of her trailer. She was something. She made these tortilla things, with cheese in the middle, and would give them to you still warm, and she pretty much never stopped talking.

Well, Mrs. Quartez vanished too, just like Mr. Romo. Like they walked out of their trailers and jumped into the sea. The Crotona police sent a car out and actually interviewed people after that. You had to be there, seriously. One thing people in Adjacent could do—our only skill, when you think about it—was BS about things we knew nothing about. Those officers heard about eighty stories and left with nothing. It didn't matter. The rest of us, us kids, we felt like the earth was moving. We thought maybe this was it. That something big was finally in the air, no matter what all the parents were saying.

Typical Adjacent, no one had any idea what was coming. How could we? It's like, how can you ever know what it feels like to be hunted, really hunted down, if it's never happened? You can't. And you can't predict anything, either, like who will keep their heads when things get seriously ugly. Which, by the way, they did.

The most twisted part of it, though, was that two kids, Lady Di Smith and Tom Jones, and this old lady friend of theirs, figured out what was happening and did something about it.

And they did it by playing with straws.

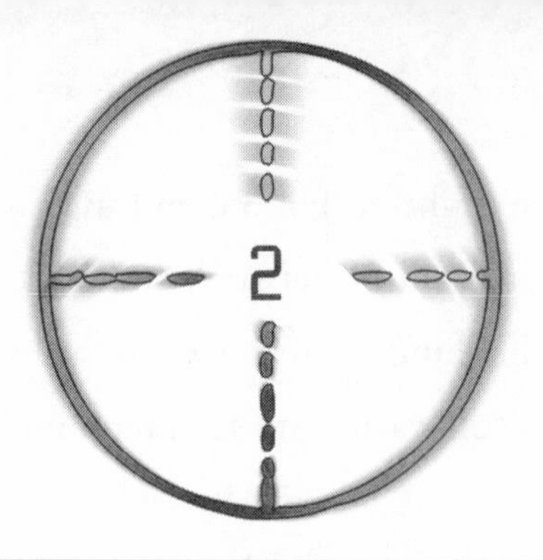

THE EMPTY TRAILER

DI'S REAL NAME WAS DIAPHANTA, OR SOMETHING LIKE that. People said she was named after an old movie star but no one knew for sure and her mom, Mrs. Smith, never said. The two Smiths lived in a small trailer near Polya's General Store, which is pretty much the center of Adjacent, so you'd see them practically every time you went to buy milk.

Di was all right, is the main thing to know. She had long, orange hair and this habit, kind of like a tic, where she kept twirling her right wrist, like she was working out a cramp or something. Everyone in Adjacent could mimic this twirling move and did so when she walked by.

They called her "Princess Di" or "Lady Di," most kids did, usually in a friendly way but sometimes not. Di didn't like it at first and told people to stop, which of course they didn't. Finally she decided it wasn't all that bad being named after Princess Diana, who was beautiful and died young.

Besides, her best friend had it worse. His full name was Tamir Abu Something Something al-Khwarizmi. Again, people didn't know for sure and didn't really ask his dad about it. They just called him Tom Jones.

No one knew what to think of Tom. He was tiny for an eleven-year-old, bony as a little bird, and you never saw his eyes. He wore this Angels baseball hat all the time, everywhere, pulled down low. He lived with his dad, Muhammad, and a bunch of younger brothers, sisters, cousins, and visiting aunts and uncles who were impossible to keep track of. He mumbled to himself a lot, Tom did, walked kind of sideways, and of course older kids wouldn't leave him alone.

That summer Di and Tom were practically dying with dread. They were about to start junior high school, taking the bus over to TriCounty Middle and High School, the huge combined school on the Crotona side of the bridge. They had heard all the stories about TriCounty—every kid does—about Crotona gangs and nasty teachers, and by August those two looked like they were walking the plank or something.

About the only thing that took their minds off of it was spending time with Malba Clarke.

Mrs. Clarke was pretty old and lived by herself. She worked nights at the plant, so she was around during most days, and during school she had kids coming by for help with homework, especially number problems. She was about a billion times better than our normal teacher, Reverend Pete, who spent nights at the bar and usually rolled into class about an hour late, mumbling and angry.

Di and Tom visited Mrs. Clarke every chance they got, and one morning they were wandering over toward her trailer. They walked in silence for a time, with Di twisting her wrist and Tom staring down at the swirls of dust in the road, shuffling along nearly sideways, like he did. They slipped under one trailer and climbed up and over a trio of beat-up units owned by Mr. Devlin, who was snoring loudly on the other side of an open window.

Mr. Devlin's hound, a ragged mutt called Noname, fell into step alongside them.

"Princess Pudgy!" some kid yelled from a window. "Where you going, piglet?"

Di didn't answer.

Somebody else yelled, "Hey, Tom, foxy hat. I think I want you."

It was still early, just after breakfast. The sun was low and warm, a maze of shadows moved across the island floor, and they could smell the sea; the greasy smell of Adjacent hadn't really hit yet.

"Do you think she's there, this early?" said Tom.

"She has to be, yeah, she should be, she probably is," said Di. "She gets home and fixes breakfast, which is kind of like her dinner, and her dinner is like her breakfast. She kind of lives backwards, I was thinking, and my theory is that maybe she's like one of those wizards in a book, you know, who starts out old and keeps getting younger."

"Why do you always have to have a theory? She just works nights, is all."

"What's wrong with having a theory? Maybe if you had more of them you wouldn't get those spaced-out crazy spells you have."

Tom stopped, pulled his hat down, and kept walking.

Mrs. Clarke lived in a deluxe unit, L-shaped with an extra room and built-in air-conditioning. She had a table and chairs in back, and always seemed to be preparing something to eat or drink for visitors.

No one could say exactly how all that homework happened in there. She'd be serving iced tea and telling some story—usually about some lunatic she knew growing up in the Pink Palace, a housing project on the far side of Crotona—and she would kind of take a break and ask, "So, what's this?" and pick one of the problems.

That's how it started. She wouldn't really give you the next chapter in the story she was telling until a problem or two got solved. And the stories were pretty good, is the thing.

Mrs. Clarke had been around, in the Navy for a while, married a Navy SEAL guy, and traveled, to places you'd heard about: Seattle. Miami. Even Washington, D.C. Just a ton of places for one person, and all real places, they were. Anyway, it was strange what happened after that. She would start telling her story again, and break again, and after a while the problems got weaved into the story somehow, and you looked up and you were done. You had figured out whatever it was you needed to.

Di, Tom, and Noname circled around the trailer, to the back patio, and saw something odd: Mrs. Clarke's patio table was out of place, and one of the chairs was lying on its side. Usually she put everything back exactly in its place, and made everyone else do the same; she was pretty insane about things like that.

The trailer was quiet, shades down, looking like its eyes were closed. Di and Tom could tell that she wasn't there. And it looked like she hadn't been around in a while.

Noname pawed at the back door, but Di and Tom stopped short.

"No! She's not there, can't you see?" Di said to the hound. "C'mon. Let's go back. Noname!"

But, typical Noname, the hound pawed crazily, he smelled something, and the door snapped open. Di and Tom didn't budge. They had spent hours on top of or under just about every trailer in Adjacent. They knew every crawl space, which ones had good hiding places and which didn't. They could disappear under a unit near the center of town and reappear almost anywhere in Adjacent. Same thing on the trailer roofs; they'd boost themselves up on a windowsill and be up and gone, moving from one roof to the next. But now suddenly they couldn't bring themselves to enter one without the owner knowing.

"Let's close the door and just go," Tom said.

Di's feet would not move. She was still staring at the ground, rocking back and forth.

"I don't know," she said. "What if something happened? Wouldn't she want us to make sure everything's OK?"

She would, Di knew. Mrs. Clarke would have said that when you can't decide whether to act or wait it is usually better to act. Acting sets the mind in motion, she would have said; and you can always change directions if you're wrong: "And searching for a solution is the best reminder that there is one." How many times had she said that?

Di looked around. They were on their own; no one was watching. Mrs. Clarke's door faced away from the central cluster of trailers, so they were out of sight of most windows.

They went in.

Noname was sniffing the floor of the kitchen. Everything was familiar and somehow alien at the same time. Mrs. Clarke's office was neat, the dishes put away, her bed made. All normal there. But something was not at all right, and Di and Tom fought the urge to run. They crept through the place almost on tiptoe, without knowing exactly why, or what they were looking for.

They found it in the kitchen. Noname was sniffing and licking some maroon spots on the tile floor. The spots trailed across the floor like spilled gravy, which Mrs. Clarke would have cleaned up immediately.

Tom dropped down on all fours. He had an idea what he was looking at but didn't want to say it out loud. Di traced the spots to the door, and saw more, trailing along the small paved patio. Her heart was working so hard now that she could feel her neck bulging and pumping. She returned to the kitchen, stood over Tom, and, turning to the hound, said, "No! What are you licking, what!"

But they knew what it was. It was blood, and it had to be Mrs. Clarke's blood. Their tutor and friend—their secret weapon, really, who was going to help them in the new school—was gone.

Mrs. Clarke was abduction number three.

THE STRAW EQUATION

THEY RAN. THEY RAN LIKE THEY WERE BEING CHASED, out toward the edge of the island, to the rusted chain-link fence that ringed the bluffs overlooking the ocean. From there they flew along the fence to the Point, a bulge of rock that hovered above the entrance to a narrow cove, about fifty yards below.

They ducked through a hole in the fence and slipped down between two boulders and into a shallow cave invisible from above. Here they had a view of the open ocean to one side, and of the cliffs dropping down to the cove on the other. They had complete privacy.

For a while they didn't speak. Breathless, the rock cold against their backs, they sat and blinked and stared. Di twirled her wrist.

Tom's eyes were huge beneath the Angels cap, and he felt a

tingling in his lower back. That was usually how it started, his waking dreamlike strangeness. The light had a liquid clarity for him now, and he could smell everything: gravel, sneakers, the surf, the ripe smell of Adjacent now stirring the air.

A swarm of ideas crowded Di's head: Maybe Mrs. Clarke was murdered, maybe kidnapped. Maybe she moved back to the Pink Palace? No, not without saying anything.

Neither one thought for a second to report what they suspected to their parents or other adults. They weren't 100 percent sure anything was wrong, for one thing. Mrs. Clarke disappeared all the time, for a few days here and there, and no one knew where she went. Same for lots of people in Adjacent, they came and went, and no one much cared. People in Adjacent didn't seem to notice much of anything. And how on earth would they explain breaking into Mrs. Clarke's trailer?

"What do we do?" said Tom. "Should we just wait, and maybe she'll come back?"

"What if she doesn't?" Di said.

Tom hung his head between his knees. "This is the worst thing ever," he said. "Worse than stupid freaking TriCounty."

"Ugh," said Di. "Don't even mention school. This is like—I mean, what happened to her? What if she's trapped or kidnapped or something, like Mr. Romo and Mrs. Quartez, and nobody does anything?"

He didn't need to answer. They stared out at the ocean for a while.

They had spent many hundreds of hours here. They could identify almost every brand of container ship that moved across the horizon—Maersk Line, Hapag-Lloyd, OOCL—as well as the yachts sailing from Crotona harbor. They had watched the garbage barges come from the city to the island dump too, so close they could identify candy wrappers, diet soda cans, Czech beer, and plastic water bottles, millions of them, with snow-capped mountain ranges on their labels.

They had imagined themselves out on those ships or yachts and had imaginary conversations, about going to Rotterdam or Hong Kong or Le Havre, the names on the ships. Now, Di thought, they might as well be on one of those garbage barges headed right back for Adjacent.

"We have to go back to her trailer," she finally said. "We have to. It's better than sitting up here and crying about it. If something bad happened to her then you just know she would have left some clue, some sign, something. Don't you think? That's my theory about it."

But Tom was already on his feet, climbing out of the cave.

Their second visit to the trailer was easier. Little time had passed since they first entered the trailer, and no one was nosing around, not even Noname or his hound friends. Not a ripple of activity disturbed the air around the unit.

Di entered first and took a position at the sink, by the

corner window. She had a clear view back toward Adjacent and was better equipped than Tom to intercept and distract any curious visitor. She was too chatty when nervous, but at least she could talk to adults. Tom was mute around anyone older than thirteen. He said very few words even to his own father, and most of those were in some Arabic language.

He was the one to look for clues, if there were any. Tom saw patterns everywhere. Geometric shapes in rock formations. Polygons and diamonds alternating in the layout of the trailer units. Colored corkscrews in the nighttime lights of Crotona. Sometimes these patterns seemed to almost glow, and he knew that the glowing somehow came from inside his head. He didn't see the world in the same way other kids did—he knew that—but there was nothing he could do about it, and he kept it to himself. He hadn't told anyone but his dad and Di.

He saw something almost immediately. Straws, on the kitchen counter, in some pattern. Mrs. Clarke used straws all the time, little stirring straws, to form equations or illustrate geometric shapes. This arrangement had to be an equation: Three straws together, followed by a space, then four straws, a saltshaker, and then five straws. She used things like saltshakers or erasers to stand for the equals sign when explaining a problem.

Di turned and noticed the straws too, and the two of them

stared at the strange arrangement for a few moments before looking at one another. Nothing. No lightning struck. Tom blinked and shrugged.

An open space for Mrs. Clarke usually meant addition. So the best first guess for the equation was: $3 + 4 = 5$.

But they had no time to meditate on it. They could hear voices outside, coming closer.

Di grabbed the straws and Tom took the shaker, and the two of them slipped out the back door and under the trailer, where they were well hidden, behind stacked garden hoses. They heard footsteps on the floor above—heavy steps, a man's.

"Malba?" It was Mr. Devlin's voice. "Malba Clarke, are you here, doll? Talk to me, now."

Di and Tom didn't make a sound. They didn't have the nerve to even look at each other. Blood, real blood, their friend's. Why would anyone hurt her? And who? What could be happening to her right now?

The straw equation seemed pretty close to nothing just then. A number riddle, an annoying puzzle, when their friend's very life was likely at risk.

Still: How could three plus four equal five?

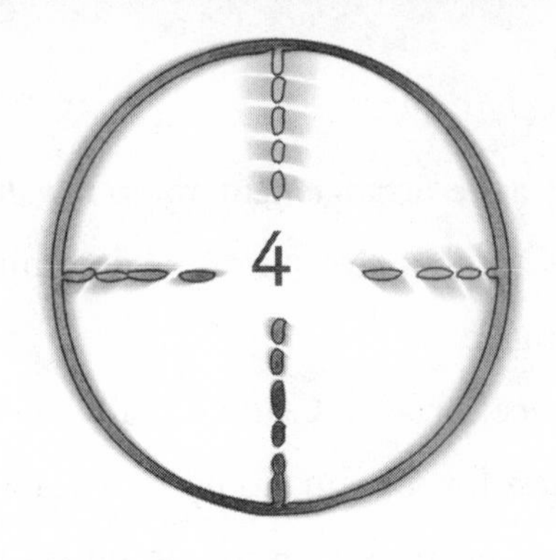

SICK STUNTS

OF COURSE NO ONE KNEW THEN HOW CRUCIAL THAT little clue would be, or how much trouble Di and Tom would find. People knew nothing, zero, about what was going on literally right beneath their feet. The plotting at the nuclear plant. The twisted plans for the island. The heinous black heart of Folsom: We were oblivious back then, like moths circling a fire.

Adjacent in August was like living on the planet Mercury or something, six blocks from the sun. The only place to hide from the heat was under the trailers with the hounds, or by the beer cooler at Polya's store before they kicked you out.

So we used to pull these sick stunts, just to forget the heat and break the dead boredom of life. Tightrope walks between trailers. Races where kids would roll down the road in old garbage cans. Or just turning on the hose and seeing who could get covered in mud fastest, and walk around like that the longest. Simple stuff, where you might get cut and bruised or beaned, but next day you were good to go.

But that summer two kids took it too far. One, Hamilton Rowan, actually tunneled through a section of Mount Trashmore on a dare.

Trashmore was the infested mountain of reeking garbage where the barges from Crotona dumped their loads. It was the gnarliest place maybe in the universe, and it changed Ham, as everyone called him. After that he lost his head entirely. He got this quiet, faraway look, and a twitch, where his head kind of jerked to one side and one of his eyes blinked.

That wasn't all, either. Theonta Hutchison, a good student and athlete, tried to water-ski behind one of the Folsom plant ferry boats to Crotona with a ski she made from a piece of plastic siding. Desperate idea.

A security guard working on a supply ferry—for Folsom, a plant security guy—he cut her rope. Insane. The currents in the channel swept Thea—that's what people called her—around to the ocean side of the island, and even now no one knows how she made it back in.

Thea got all silent too, like Ham, and said she was dropping out of school. That hit people kind of hard, because she was big and strong and smart and kids idolized her a little. Still, the news about Mrs. Clarke spread fast, in the usual Adjacent way. Mr. Devlin told someone, who told someone, and three seconds later Mrs. Polya had it. She was the newscast. She knew everybody and talked to people when they came into her store to make sure they were up to date.

Not like most parents cared that much, about Mrs. Clarke or anything else. Maybe it was because Mrs. Clarke was smart, and kind of pretty for an older lady, and had some fancy technical job at the plant. Or because she would talk to some of the most twisted characters around. Like Big Sip, this fat bum who wandered around with a giant cup of soda and mostly grunted at people. Or even Blue Moon, a giant, scary old surfer who lived out by the cliffs. Bip Sip could barely talk and Blue Moon was either a convict or an escaped mental patient as far as anyone knew.

Anyway, parents kind of shrugged and had this opinion that Mrs. Clarke was a little off anyway, so most likely she just picked up and moved on. And that was that. No detectives, no police, no citizen search parties or anything, like on TV. People thought it was nothing.

Well, we knew better, and so did Di and Tom. This was not random, especially after Mr. Romo and Mrs. Quartez. And pretty soon we had all the evidence we needed. One afternoon, totally out of nowhere, a security guard showed up in Adjacent. A few days after the Mrs. Clarke news got out, there he was: a hard-looking hombre, with a uniform and an official Folsom Energy badge, pilot sunglasses, the whole costume. He parked his jeep right near Mrs. Clarke's place, and put ribbons of that yellow police tape around the trailer. It looked pretty hilarious and kind of spooky at the same time, to be honest about it.

Again, it should have freaked out everyone: a guard from the plant. No one could remember seeing anything like it. When had anyone ever been interested in anything in Adjacent? Not since ever, is when. And it wasn't like he just sat there, looking tough. He started talking to people. Investigating. Asking around about who had been in Mrs. Clarke's trailer. And one day Monte Gaspard, this other kid, saw the guard beat his hound with a chain bicycle lock. His own hound, and Gas (that's what we called him) said the hound was whimpering and bleeding. It was just a matter of time before he got to Di and Tom.

But the first Adjacent local to really catch a whiff that those two were up to something was Mrs. Smith. She woke up late at night to find her daughter out on the front steps, with a math textbook on her lap. On the ground at her feet was a scattering of straws. Mrs. Smith was preparing to be annoyed but the sight of the schoolbook stopped her. She opened the trailer door delicately, so as not to interrupt the studying.

"Di?" she said. "Are you preparing for—"

Di cut her off: "Mom? Can you look at this? Is it possible that three plus four equals five?"

Mrs. Smith sat down on the step next to her daughter, and pulled a cinnamon stick from her pocket and stuck it in her mouth; she was trying to quit smoking, using sticks instead of smokes. It seemed impossible to her that she would ever succeed. She had been taking extra shifts at the plant, cleaning work, and some data entry jobs, and barely had time to get breakfast and dinner made.

She saw that Di was tracing the equation in the dirt.

"Um, let's see, honey," she said. As a girl she had been desperate in math and science, and it occurred to Mrs. Smith suddenly that no one had sat down with her like this, ever, over a problem. This one looked kind of easy, yet she felt a ripple of fear when she saw she had no idea where to start.

The two of them sat there under the porch light for a while. Di had spent hours counting and recounting, trying subtraction, multiplication, and division with combinations of three, four, and five. She was close to giving up. Now she was simply playing with the straws, using them to make shapes.

"Look, I almost have something," she said. She had six of Mrs. Clarke's straws on the ground in a rough circle, a hexagon. She had placed a straw at each joint, upright, coming together at a point above the ground, forming a kind of pyramid.

"Di, honey, I'm thrilled you're working on puzzles, but what is this about?" Mrs. Smith finally said.

"Wait. One second," her daughter said. She now had the

straws in a triangle, lying flat on the ground, three on one side, four on another, and five straws on the third side. "Huh. That's something, isn't it? It doesn't look like much, but at least it fits."

Mrs. Smith blinked at her daughter, yawned. "And?" she said. She got no answer. The girl was too absorbed, fiddling with the straw triangle, staring at it intensely.

"Right," Mrs. Smith said. "OK, well, I'm going back to bed. But I want to hear about this tomorrow."

Tom, who was also up late that night, had no explaining to do. His pa was used to him being up at all hours, working on homework, listening to music on his radio, or just staring into the sky. Tom's dad knew that his son's mind wheeled way off sometimes and created things others couldn't see.

Tom's dad didn't make a big deal out of it, though. Sometimes he asked his son what he was thinking and they would talk about it in Arabic, and Mr. Muhammad—that's what everyone called him—he would kind of shake his head and smile like he wished he could see it all. Which he did wish, no doubt. But Tom kind of worried him a little too, you could see that.

Tom had found some stirring straws of his own, and was playing with them. But mostly he just fed the numbers three, four, and five into his brain and sat back and watched what happened.

He felt the tingling in his lower back and then his head swirled with all kinds of shapes with three, four, and five sides.

Squares that expanded and shrunk and turned around before the four sides fell apart and reassembled into something else: a triangle, a diamond, then a star. Sides were added or subtracted as needed, in sets of three, four, and five. The shapes turned more and reassembled into three dimensions. Boxes. Pyramids.

It was well after midnight when he thought he saw something that had to do with squares.

It was this:

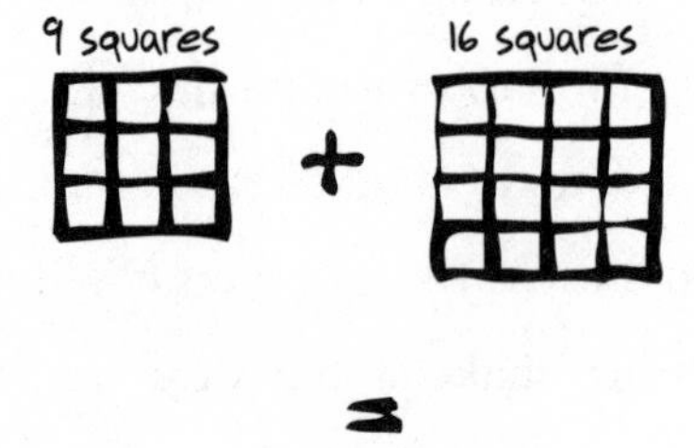

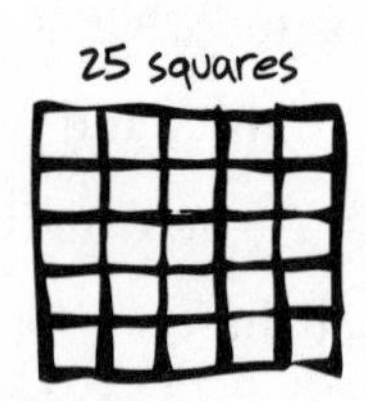

If you took a square with three straws on each side, and then combined that with a four-straw square, you got a bigger square (of course) that looked like it might be equal in size to a square with five straws on each side.

Or at least pretty close. Tom pulled out some graph paper

and drew a quick picture: He counted the squares inside the two smaller squares and, sure enough, they added up to the boxes inside the larger one. The three-by-three square had nine boxes. The four-by-four one had sixteen boxes. The five-by-five had twenty-five. And 9 + 16 = 25. Could that be something?

It must be. It was. He needed to talk to Di.

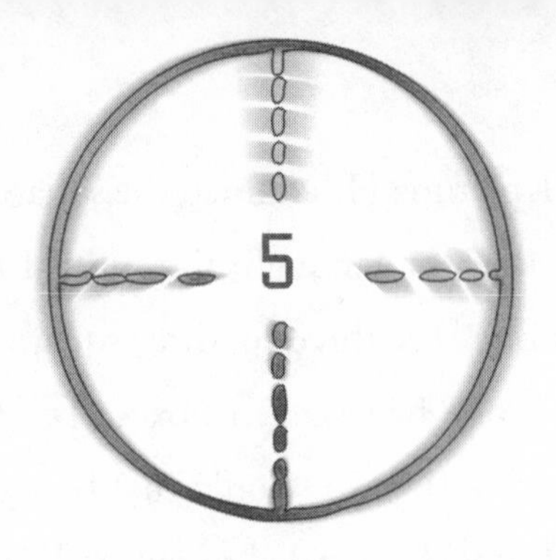

THE SILVER TRIANGLE

THEY MET EARLY THE NEXT DAY, AS USUAL, JUST AFTER breakfast. Morning was their time, had been ever since Di first saw Tom outside just after dawn one day when she was seven, walking over to Polya's for milk. Normally, the only people ever out of bed at that hour were nightshift workers returning home and drunks coming out of the Broken Bamboo bar, like zombies from *Night of the Living Dead.* One of them, Charlie Rowan—Ham's dad—zigzagged out into the road that day and face-planted into the dust, his wallet popping out of his back pocket. He was just lying there in the road where a car could easily squash him, and Di stopped outside the store, afraid to go too close.

She saw a boy with a red hat move out of the shadows, pick up the man's wallet, and hold it out to him. Mr. Rowan lunged and took a swipe at the boy from the ground—Mr. Rowan was a lunatic, even when he wasn't drunk—and the boy just stood there and waited and then placed the wallet next to Mr. Rowan's hand and disappeared. Mr. Rowan picked the thing up and crawled out of the road.

Di kept an eye out for the red hat after that and noticed that the boy would hang around the Quartez trailer, where adults and kids always gathered around lunchtime to play cards, gossip, and yell at each other to turn their radios down. Mrs. Quartez always had something going on the grill. Mr. Devlin would be there, chewing on a giant cigar—never smoking it, probably because he only had that one. Those were the deep-down Adjacent locals right around Mrs. Quartez, and Di saw the boy there, on the edges, just watching. He looked very uncertain, but held his ground there, Di saw, like a little kid on the high dive, not yet ready to dive but determined not to climb down.

"Hey," she said to him one day. "You wanna go climb on the old buses in the bus graveyard behind the store? I know how to get in one."

The boy looked down at his feet, nodded his cap, and off they went. She blabbed so much on the way over to the buses that Tom smiled once and said, "I see cool stuff." It was the first thing he ever told her, that he had strange visions, mostly because it was the only thing he could think to say. He had to say something; the orange-haired girl was saying too much and he wanted a break.

They had the mornings to themselves pretty much ever since.

When they met on this morning, they chose their path carefully. They did not dare go over to the Point; the route was too easily visible from Mrs. Clarke's trailer. They headed the opposite direction, stopped off at Polya's Grocery for two cream sodas and BBQ sunflower seeds, and struck out from there, across the plant road and inland, back toward the bus graveyard.

The bus graveyard was basically a pile of old buses, just outside of town. School buses mainly, some rusted, some crawling with lizards, and a couple of them burned out. An Adjacent landmark if ever there was one. You could climb around in that pile if you knew where you were going.

Di and Tom had one bus they liked best, a junked luxury liner with squishy seats. They could climb up into this bus and if they needed to disappear—like, if some older kid was looking for them—they could slip through this trapdoor in the floor and into the luggage compartment underneath.

They propped themselves on seats near the front and Di laid out her straws. It was her best idea, the 3-4-5 triangle. The only way she could get three and four to somehow combine to equal five.

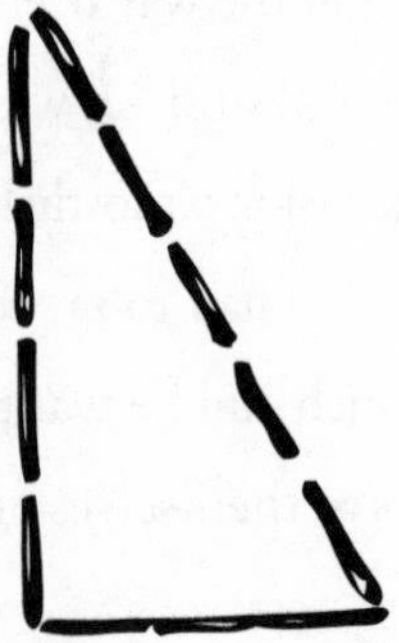

They stared at the shape for a while, waiting for it to tell them something, like a secret code, like in the movies.

Nothing happened. The straws just lay there on the seat, looking exactly like straws on the seat of an old bus.

A breath of wind came through the bus in a low whistle, and the light changed outside somehow. Neither one said a word but they both suddenly had a strange feeling, a light-headed sensation.

Di straightened up and began to pace the tilted bus aisle. She was talking to herself, in a rising, anxious voice. "What did she say? What DID she say, what did she SAY, whatdidshesay, WHATdidshesay?"

She stopped and stared at Tom. "She said it, Mrs. Clarke did, remember? Just the last time we were there? She said this was a special kind of triangle. A triangle where the sides add up if the sides are all squares. She said that. I remember it because I thought it sounded crazy, like, are we talking about triangles or squares here?"

Tom was still staring at the figure, and in the strange light coming through the tinted bus windows he thought he saw a silvery glint on the straw triangle. Impossible to tell if his mind was playing tricks on him. Sometimes when he saw colors it meant something was clicking into place, and sometimes it was just him seeing things.

He remembered now. Mrs. Clarke had said a lot about this

kind of triangle: a *right* triangle, she called it. If you multiplied the length of each short side times itself—3 × 3 and 4 × 4—and added them together, it equaled the long side times itself: 5 × 5. Just like the squares he had drawn. Not only that, Mrs. Clarke had said that this was true *for every triangle like this ever made.* Always and everywhere. Then he saw it. It was so completely simple, so stupidly obvious. The 3 × 3 and 4 × 4 were squares.

They were exactly the squares he had been combining in his head the night before. The one with three straws per side and the other with four:

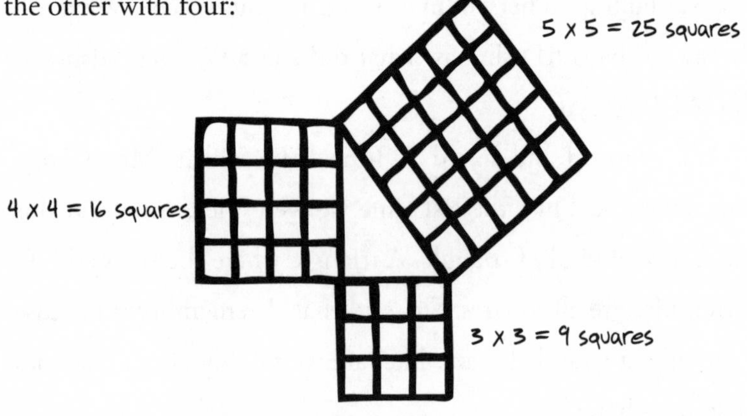

"This is it, Di, this is it. This is what she wanted us to get, this has to be!" Now the thing with Tom, he hardly ever smiled, really smiled. But when he did it was something, because his grin was way too big for his tiny head. Seriously, you had to see it, and it was a miracle that Di kept a straight face watching him. Anyone else would have fallen on her head laughing.

But she didn't, and Tom bounced up on one of the chairs, kneeled in front of a window, and did a muscleman pose.

"What!?" Di yelled. Di had never seen him do anything like it and assumed his mind was floating again.

She stared at him for a moment before noticing that she was kind of hugging herself. It was an unusual sensation, whatever it was, and not at all bad. She thought for a second maybe this is what it felt like to figure out something, even though this was almost nothing, just a simple triangle rule. It wasn't like they'd derived some big math rule or anything; she knew that. But still. This was a real clue, and they both knew it.

The two of them lingered there for a while, until Tom dropped his arms.

"OK, now what?" he said.

"I have an idea," Di said. "But it means we have to go back to Mrs. Clarke's place."

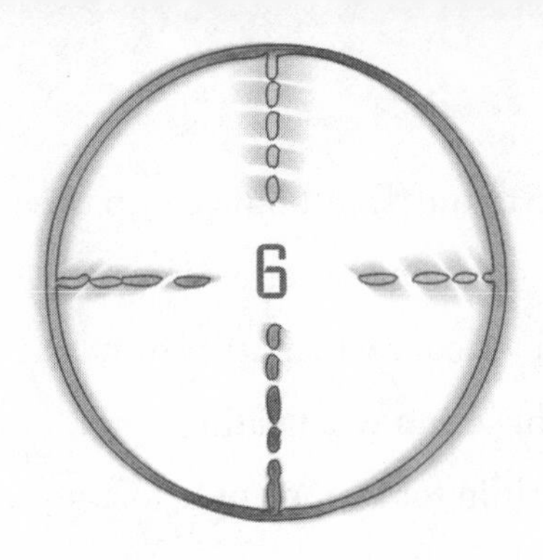

6 SULLEN HILLBILLIES

ONE THING YOU COULD SAY ABOUT ADJACENT, DEAD lame as it was: It had some hiding places. Old cars, sitting on blocks in people's yards. Rusted-out vans, turning red-black in the sun. The bus graveyard. Roofs too, and the alleyways between trailers, and of course the crawl spaces, little storage areas underneath some trailers, where people stashed engine parts and tools, tarps, hoses, anything. Some kids had dug out entire forts down there, big holes with plywood roofs, and you could sleep in there. People did it too. In the dark, forget it. You could vanish. Down and under the trailers, or up and onto the roofs, and you were into the maze. Gone. A good thing too, because Adjacent had some of the cruelest clowns known to man, who hunted down younger kids for fun. More on those twisted pigs later. The point was, Adjacent kids already had some idea of what it was like to be tracked down.

But this was different, what was happening now with this security man. People made fun of him and imitated the way he walked around and stared and everything. But he was all business. Whatever he was doing, he was serious and determined, and those were two things that people in Adjacent were not at all. He actually moved into Mrs. Clarke's trailer, like it was his. The sick thing about this was, no one stopped him, or said anything. They just accepted it, him moving right into Mrs. Clarke's trailer. Think of some stranger moving into your own trailer, sleeping on the couch, and your parents don't throw him out—that's what it felt like.

This being Adjacent, he got mostly bad information or none at all. Most people would not talk to anyone official looking, no matter who they were. But someone must have said something, because he was starting to ask around about any kids who might have visited Mrs. Clarke's trailer, or went there for help with homework. There weren't that many of those, maybe eight or ten, and Di and Tom had a sense they were being watched.

Di's plan was simple. They would visit Mrs. Clarke's trailer and have another look around. The triangle rule was not enough; it needed to be connected to something real. Di reasoned backward: The question they were trying to answer was, where? Where was Mrs. Clarke? So, for any clue to be useful, it had to give a location—a specific place.

"That's my theory, and if you've got a better one then let me know, OK? And don't say anything about theories, either, because this is serious now."

Tom Jones didn't. He liked her theory.

They met early the next morning, in front of Polya's. They stole toward Mrs. Clarke's trailer, staying low, moving under trailers, steering clear of yards with hounds. The sky was low and misty, the floor of the island still swirling in pools of gray. They found the blinds down on Mrs. Clarke's trailer, and no light behind them, no movement. Impossible to tell if he was up, or even inside. The trailer, so familiar to them, was now an alien outpost, possessed.

They moved right up next to it without a sound, still too sleepy to worry about being caught, and dropped underneath.

Mrs. Clarke kept her crawl space cleaner than most did, and she had several rolled-up tarps down there where Di and Tom could wedge themselves and be entirely out of sight.

They lay there and listened, hearing only their own breath. Di felt her heartbeat in her neck, and a tingling, secret-agent sensation. Amazingly, she hadn't thought about TriCounty Middle and High School all morning, and it usually festered in her mind like a wound that wouldn't heal.

Nothing seemed to move in the trailer; still no sound. They both began to wonder if the guard had gone, or if he was asleep.

The two of them were so unsure of their next move and lying so still that they would have fallen back asleep if they hadn't been so wired. But the shadows around them seemed to evaporate suddenly, and Di knew they had to do something soon. If they lingered too long here they would not be able to escape unseen once Adjacent was awake and the people were up and about.

Tom put his head up first, and nodded to Di. He slid like a snake over to the side opposite the trailer's bedroom, and poked his head out.

Still no sound, no movement from the trailer. Di then saw Tom slip out, and up—his feet disappeared—and he was gone. He had climbed up on top of the unit.

She followed, pulling herself out, and then climbing quickly, using the drainpipe and a windowsill, her sneaker giving a soft squeak that made her heart stall. She froze and listened; nothing. She peeked over at Tom Jones and saw that he was as excited as she was. Di finally sat up and was looking around when a screeching noise split the air, and then a crack—the back door.

The two of them held their breath again. Tom gave a bug-eyed look. Di became light-headed, the whole earth seemed to tilt a half turn, and she held her breath to keep from collapsing in nervous laughter.

The guard was just below them!

In back of the trailer, out of sight, but they could smell his cigarette, hear the mumble of his voice. Were there two of them? They didn't dare peek, not yet. They believed with every naked cell in their entire bodies that they were about to be caught, and sentenced to hours or even days of miserable explaining to parents, maybe moving boxes at Polya's or sweeping the floor at the Bamboo, which smelled so bad it gave you a headache. Yet they were still out of sight, and the guard—they could hear his voice more clearly now—was pacing in the back. He was talking on a cell phone.

"Nothing so far, for certain, sir," they heard him saying, in a high voice; annoyingly high. "No . . . no . . . there's nothing here. I've ransacked the place . . . that's right . . . and it could be kids. Yeah, she was some kind of teacher, she tutored them or something. It's hard to tell, though. No one here is telling me much. Bunch of sullen hillbillies, guns and prayers and no education type of thing. But I'll find who was here and where they put the drive. Trust me on that."

He hung up and went back inside. Di and Tom still hadn't moved. They were as dead still as a pair of desert lizards and again listened to every creak, every whisper from the trailer, and soon heard a hissing sound.

Di relaxed; so did Tom. It was the shower.

Di, staring back toward central Adjacent, watched as the low sun warmed the roofs of the trailers. She gasped. Pointed. Whispered: "Tom, look. The red roof! That's it. See? How she, Mrs. Clarke, always pointed out her window to explain stuff, and would say it was three hundred yards to the red roof? Well, there it is!"

They now had a clean view, and there was no question: The red roof belonged to the Kroneckers, near the middle of Adjacent. It was three hundred yards to the red roof, Mrs. Clarke had said, and she had always told them to connect shapes and lines and numbers to real things. And when she did so herself, she almost always spoke in terms of yards. Di could hear her words: "The three, four, and five are not just numbers on paper but real distances, like three hundred, four hundred, and five hundred yards." Now, they had connected the numbers to real things. It wasn't for sure but it felt right: The line from Mrs. Clarke's to the Kroneckers' was one of the three sides of the 3-4-5 triangle.

They slid down, on the side opposite the shower, and moved away, casual and slow at first and then at a dead sprint. They thought they heard the guard yell something but by then they had disappeared into the dark maze of trailers at the edge of Adjacent, and into a crawl space, to rest.

"You know where to go next?" Di said, showing a hyena grin.

"Yes. And we're going to find something there."

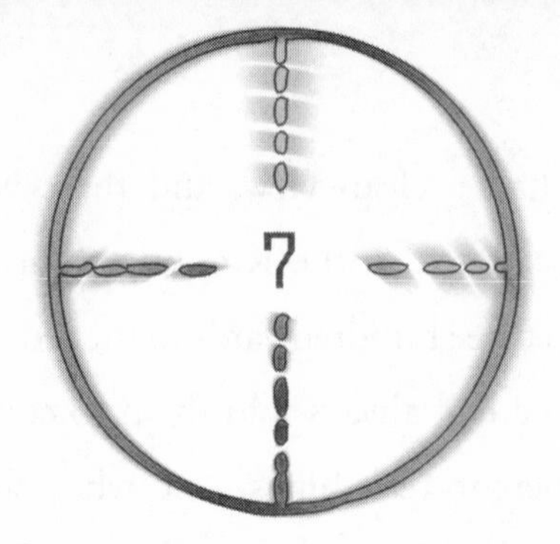

THE OUTHOUSES

THEY WERE BREATHING HARD, AND STARVING, BY the time they arrived at Polya's. They didn't need to talk about what to buy; they split up and Tom got a package of cream cakes while Di picked up the BBQ sunflower seeds and cream sodas. They put the items on Mrs. Smith's tab.

"What are you two up to, out of breath this early?" said Mrs. Polya. "What mysteries are you trying to solve?"

"Uh, hello, Mrs. Pol—nothing. Seriously."

Di and Tom devoured the cream cakes in two bites and practically skipped over to the Kroneckers'. They yelled hello to Big Sip, who was out in the road, drawing circles in the dirt, like he sometimes did. They waved to Mrs. Smith and her friends, who were out drinking coffee on Di's steps.

They knew that a yard was about three feet long, or roughly

one long step. They knew that the distance from Mrs. Clarke's to the Kroneckers' was three hundred yards—the "3" side of the triangle. And they knew that, in order to match the 3-4-5 right triangle, they would have to trace a line that crossed the line from Mrs. Clarke's to the Kroneckers' squarely, like a plus sign. The triangle could only go one of two ways: to the left of the Kroneckers' four hundred yards on a straight line, or to the right four hundred yards.

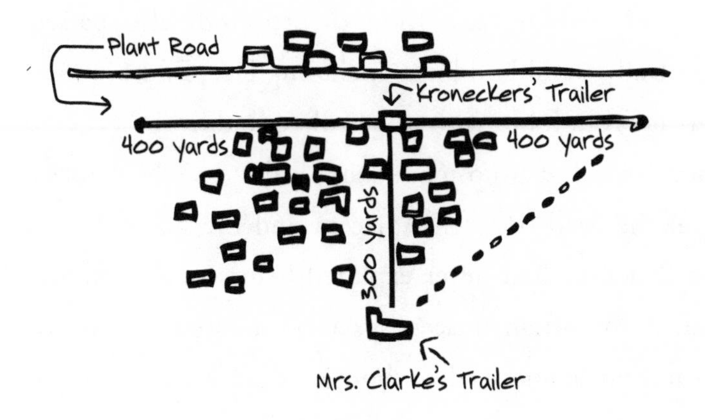

They eyeballed the angle and started counting off steps from the Kroneckers' trailer. If the distance was three hundred yards from Mrs. Clarke's, they would have to go four hundred yards, four hundred long steps, to find the third point in the triangle.

But which way?

They decided to go left first, away from the plant. They duckwalked along a line parallel to the road. The line cut through some trailers and buildings, and ended up at the trailer where Monte Gaspard (Gas) lived. No crawl space; no hiding places; and Gas had about ten younger brothers and sisters who were swarming the place, as Mrs. Gas was yelling and trying to fix breakfast.

"You thinking what I'm thinking?" Di said.

"Yeah. Not a chance. Should we try the other way?"

The line running east from the red roof also passed through trailers and buildings, including DeepEnd Liquors, and Di and Tom followed it as best they could.

They arrived at a no-man's-land, a flat stretch of rocky earth off the road between Adjacent and the plant. It was a place that they had never explored before or even much noticed. A forgotten, unseen space on a forgotten island. A few ancient abandoned outhouses stood watch over the empty stretch, reeking as if they were still in use.

Di and Tom held their noses and looked for something, anything that could be a clue.

Di was shaking her head and circling her wrist, and she groaned loudly. "This is nothing! What is this? I thought we had it. Why, why, why?!"

She reddened, caught her breath, cringed. "Ugh, someone

exploded a turd bomb in this place. Ohhh, Tom, what were we thinking? Stupid right triangle! Oh, I can't stand this. What are we doing out here?!"

Tom, determined to appear brave, forced himself to look inside one of the outhouses. The smell dropped him to one knee, a mix of toilet sewage and chemicals. The toilet was filled with junk, cans and toilet paper and cigarette butts, an ancient garbage can. He went to the next one, and found the same thing; his stomach began to burn. The third outhouse, however, did not stink. There wasn't even a toilet, only an empty hole. He stared at the hole, and without thinking much about it, put his head down into it. Total darkness. An unusual smell too. Cool and dank. The smell of open space.

He blinked, and blinked some more. When his eyes adjusted to the darkness he saw a cave—no, a room—a man-made opening with a small ladder going down. He almost fell in trying to see the bottom of the ladder.

He called out "Di!" and climbed in.

Di heard the thrill in his voice and stopped yelling. She was right behind him, climbing down the ladder. They stepped carefully off the last rung and let a foot slide down to a solid floor, which was still too dark to see. They stood at the foot of the ladder for a while, hanging on to it, breathing in the cool humming silence, which seemed a million miles from the heat, noise, and smell of Adjacent.

After a while their eyes adjusted to the ghostly, deep-gray light: It was a small room, all right, dusty and unused. A secret underground room! No one they knew had ever been down here; they were sure of it. On the wall to their left was a control panel of some kind, with a few buttons and dials, almost invisible beneath black soot.

The floor felt sharply tilted. It was hard to stand. They soon saw why: They were standing on top of a giant pipe, most of which was below the floor. Another massive pipe crossed it like a plus sign; there was room to stand beside the pipes, but not much. Dropping to a crouch, they moved slowly to search the place. Tom slipped to the far wall and into the pooling darkness, gone; Di said his name just to be sure and he said, "I'm here. At the wall. It's only a few feet away."

"OK. I just couldn't see you." Di crawled directly over one of the pipes, down the middle of the space, and saw something right near where the two huge cylinders crossed: a few more dials, dirty, broken, like the others. But just past those there was something else, something whitish, right where the two pipes intersected. They were numbers.

"Tom."

He came over immediately. "What?"

They gawked for a time, as if to be sure they weren't imagining things in the dark. But they weren't. Someone had clearly written two pairs of numbers in chalk:

0, 0

-12, 8

A knot of horror and delight uncoiled in that small dark space. Di and Tom knew in their bones that Mrs. Clarke had written those numbers. They recognized the squat ovals of the zeros. Their right triangle solution had not been stupid. It had been correct! No other explanation remotely made sense.

They were meant to see these numbers—but what were they?

"Here we go again," Di said.

Tom didn't say anything. He was lost in thought, now seated on the shoulder of one of the pipes. Di sat down on the other pipe, checked the chalk numbers again, and wondered what they could mean. She had no ideas and decided to simply sit there for a moment and take in the room. Her eyes were still adjusting, as were her other senses. She noticed that the faint hum that she thought was the absence of sound seemed to grow. The hum was deeper, and then louder, and now louder still. Tom finally looked up.

Something was moving toward them, and suddenly the growling horrible mouth of it seemed to sweep toward the room. Thunder, a rolling wave of sound—what?—like some underground freight train was barreling at them.

Whatever it was rumbled right through the pipe Tom was sitting on, and the massive cylinder groaned and bucked—throwing Tom hard to the floor, and Di too. Down and scrambling along the floor like insects toward the walls of the room. Tom found a crack in the wall, and disappeared into it. He had always assumed that his life would end when one of the bigger kids who taunted him cornered him for real, with no one around. He now thought this was it: He was going to die in some weird earthquake under an outhouse.

The room shook like it was going to fall to pieces for what seemed like a very long time. No one could hear Tom's and Di's screams, not even them. The thunder buried everything with its sound.

And then, just like that, it stopped.

Trembling badly, Di and Tom crawled back toward the ladder. Di's hands were shaking so much she had trouble grabbing the bars. They climbed out of the room as if out of the grave, and tumbled out of the outhouse and into the bright sun. Their ears were ringing so severely that they couldn't hear themselves speak. They lay there in the gravel for a while, waiting to feel normal. Di closed her eyes and felt the warm sun on her face and let the chalk numbers play through her head: 0, 0 and 12, 8.

She stared at those figures running across the back of her eyelids and imagined them in colors, like she knew Tom would. Tom had told her about that: Color them. Brand them. Burn them into your brain. Let the even numbers be cool as the morning tide, midnight blues and seaweed green; the odd ones run warm, like sand and bamboo and the red-orange neon sign over DeepEnd Liquors. The twelve might even be a negative number; it looked like there was a little dash in front of it.

They jogged back toward Adjacent, light-headed, almost skipping, loose and silly and oblivious as a couple of kindergartners kicking an old soda can. Their heads were swimming with the numbers—two zeros (silver white), a two (powder blue), the eight (purple black), the one as orange as a stove light—and there wasn't room for much else.

Their stomachs were dead empty, though. Di knew there were hot dogs in the fridge, and a jar of sweet pickles too. She could taste those already. Maybe, Di thought, her mom had even come home for lunch and would make everything for them. Right now, more than ever, they deserved that.

Di pushed through her trailer door, with Tom right

behind her, and practically knocked her mom over—she was home!

But there was a guilty scared look on her face, and Di turned to see two men in the room. One was a short, soft-looking man with a pink face and a pair of wire glasses. He looked like a cartoon mayor, or a professor.

The other man was the security guard.

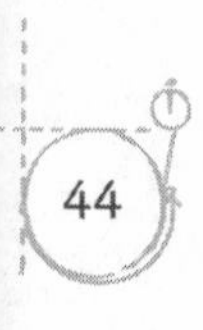

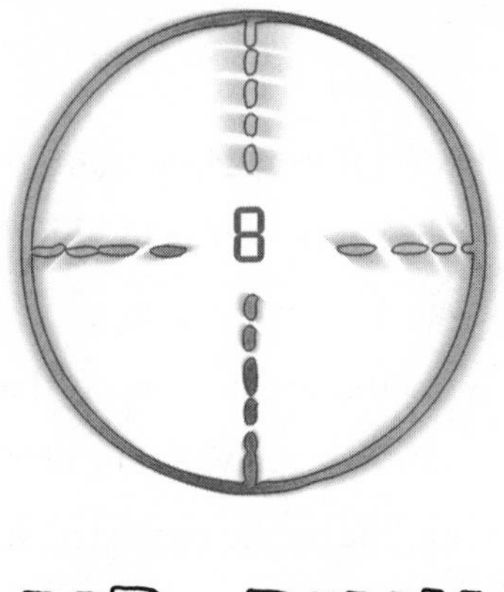

8

MR. PINK

DI HAD A NOTION TO RUN, BUT THE SHORT, PINK MAN held a finger up, and a momentary glimmer of anger showed in his eyes. Tom, standing in the doorway, froze too.

"Hold that thought, young woman," he said, now smiling kindly. "We come in peace. I am an executive at the Folsom plant, and I believe you're already acquainted with my colleague here, Mr. Brown. We're very worried about what is going on in this community. We depend on Folsom Adjacent, and we're here to find out what's going on. We're here to help." He glanced back at Mrs. Smith, at Mr. Brown, and back at Mrs. Smith.

"Now, ma'am, we'd like to speak to your daughter and her friend in private, if that's OK with you. We'll only be a few minutes. You may wait outside, and I assure you, everything is fine. We have been interviewing many of the children in town, and everyone has been very helpful."

Di hated the way he said "children," like he was talking about puppies or something. She noticed that Mr. Pink had a mole near his ear, with hair growing out of it. Long hairs. You could practically braid them, she thought. No, you *could* braid them.

Mrs. Smith gave her daughter a look and then stepped out of the trailer; Di noticed she had cigarettes with her.

"Now," the man said, once he had closed the door. "Let's have a conversation, shall we?" The easiness was gone from his voice.

"Mr. Brown here, as I imagine you know, has been investigating some of the disappearances here on the island."

Some of the disappearances? thought Di. Why not all of them? She peeked over at Tom but his face was invisible beneath the Angels hat. That's what happened when he was scared: He shrunk, literally; his face disappeared.

"Mr. Brown has been asking around about your friend, Mrs. Clarke," Mr. Pink continued. "We want to find Mrs. Clarke too, and we know that she was your friend. She helped you in math, isn't that right? Well, we are interviewing everyone who knew her, to try to find out what happened to her. Do you follow me?" He suddenly looked kindly again, an affectionate uncle Joe.

Di hated the tone of his voice now, like he was talking to three-year-olds.

"Yes, yeah, I mean we follow, sure," she said. Tom nodded his cap very slightly.

"Good. Now, it's very important that this conversation is between us. Do not tell your parents. If you do, we'll find out, and we will make things hard for you. And for them. Understood?"

They nodded again. The fear Di had been holding down by being annoyed now seeped back. One thing every kid in Adjacent learned at an early age was what a threat sounded like. The trailer, the only home Di had ever known, seemed suddenly unfamiliar, cramped, too hot.

Mr. Pink glanced over his shoulder at Mr. Brown, and again looked closely at Di and Tom. His face was gentle again, his eyes warming. This back and forth between hard guy and good neighbor was becoming exhausting.

"Now then. Have either one of you been over to Mrs. Clarke's trailer in the past few weeks?"

Di and Tom were afraid to look at each other, and suddenly weren't completely sure they should breathe. Mr. Pink's manner and confidence made it seem almost certain that he knew the answer to all his questions already. Worse than that, Di thought, he might even be able to read her thoughts.

Her head was now so hot it throbbed. She thought it would

be impossible to try to lie to this man, and decided all at once to tell him everything. About the straws, the cave, the triangle, all of it.

Yet when she opened her mouth to begin pouring it all out, she heard, as if from a great distance, only two words: "No, sir."

She couldn't remember the last time she'd said so few words in one breath.

Mr. Pink's face lost its color, moved in closer. "You're absolutely sure? You didn't go visit your friend, at all?"

Mr. Brown cleared his throat. "And you haven't been playing in the caves, or at the dump over by—"

Here Mr. Pink turned quickly and shot a look at Mr. Brown that made the security guard swallow his words.

"Yes, sir, I'm sure," she said. Tom signaled his agreement. If he shrunk any more he'd be nothing but a pile of clothes. Mr. Pink took a step back, and sighed. A breath of air seemed to enter the room, as if the trailer sighed with him.

Mr. Brown, who was leaning on the kitchen counter, straightened up and spoke. "Please come to me if you hear any information from anyone," he said.

Di opened her mouth to answer but a loud knocking at the door stopped her. Mrs. Smith pushed through the door, with a desperate look in her eyes.

"Is everything OK here? Di? Sir? I have to get back to work," she said, shooting a worried and suspicious look toward Di. Di almost threw herself into her mother's arms she was so relieved to see her. In the fever of the last few minutes she had forgotten that her mom was waiting outside the trailer; she had forgotten anything outside the trailer existed.

"Excuse us, ma'am, you've been very patient," Mr. Pink said, sounding kindly again, and putting a hand on Mrs. Smith's shoulder, as if reassuring an old friend. "I want to thank you. Your daughter and her friend have been polite and helpful, and that can only be the reflection of a good home. I would be happy to take you back to the plant. I'll just step outside and have a quick word with Mr. Brown first, if you'll permit us."

Mrs. Smith nodded, and then put her arm around her daughter's shoulders.

"Hey, you, is everything all right?" she said. "Tell me what's happening."

Di said, "Sure, OK, yeah, Mom, it's good," as sweetly as she could and tried not to cry.

Tom was beginning to cry a little under his hat and excused himself to go to the bathroom, to hide. He closed the door, and stood on the toilet and stared out the tiny bathroom window above. He desperately wanted to be out at the Point, or in the bus graveyard: somewhere, anywhere else, far away from the two men. He knew there was no real escape, ever—this was Adjacent—and he was just about to step down when he heard voices.

Below the window, there they were, talking, nearly mumbling, in what passed for the back patio of the Smiths' unit. Tom could hear every word.

"No, sir, I couldn't tell for certain, it's very hard to with kids," the security man was saying. "They could be lying, or just nervous, or even making stuff up. But I'll watch them. I know I saw someone prowling around the caves."

Mr. Pink then said something Tom couldn't hear; he only saw Mr. Brown's face freeze with fear.

TRICOUNTY

SUMMERS IN ADJACENT DIDN'T EXACTLY MELT AWAY into colorful falls, with leaf piles and touch football and Christmas sales. There were no trees, for one thing. No grass fields or stores, either, at least not the kind you always see on TV, and it didn't even get that much colder in the fall. Normally Di and Tom would have been out at the Point during the last days of summer, staring out at the sea, desperately counting every last minute. Not now. Their heads were so full of zeroes, eights, and twelves that they lost track of time altogether.

They would meet early at Polya's, pool their money, buy cream sodas, BBQ sunflower seeds, and cream cakes, and find a quiet piece of ground, usually near Tom's trailer. They drew diagrams in the dirt, using the numbers and anything else they had—sticks, stones, marbles, straws. The lucky straws. Di had saved all of them and stashed them in the back of a drawer under her bed, like a secret treasure.

For instance, with 12 and 8, you could divide both by 4 and get 3 and 2, respectively. Adding 3 and 2 gave you 5. A pentagon had five sides. Multiplying 3 and 2 gave you 6; and if you added up all the numbers that divided into 6 (1 + 2 + 3), they also equaled 6. Hmm, thought Di. What did that mean?

Probably nothing.

Tom had been up late nights again, watching the numbers 12 and 8 turn and shape-shift in his head. Once he thought he saw something, in the number 128. He divided it into four pieces: 2, 7, 21, and 98. Something strange happened when he multiplied, added, subtracted, and divided each of these numbers by 7. Here's what he found:

$2 \times 7 = 14$

$7 + 7 = 14$

$21 - 7 = 14$

$98 \div 7 = 14$

He stared at that for a while and couldn't believe it worked out that way. Always 14. But so what?

And then one afternoon they looked up and saw that the empty afternoons were over. The summer collapsed into a final, gloomy Saturday and a death march Sunday toward the one thing Di and Tom suddenly feared far more than the security man or Mr. Pink: TriCounty Middle and High School.

In truth, that morning—the first day of school—didn't feel that much different than any other first day. The younger kids going to TriCounty for the first time waved to their parents and stared at the ground and stood with frozen smiles, waiting for the bus near Polya's. Ham Rowan—the twisted lunatic who tunneled through Mount gnarly Trashmore—was there in the lot too, off by himself, looking lost. And Adjacent's twin terrors, the *real* biohazards on the island, were lurking: Rene D. Quartez, smooth and bald and angry-looking as always, was talking with his friend, Pascal Blasé, fat and dangerous, with blond dreadlocks and his usual crooked smile. If Rene D. always looked like he wanted to murder someone, Pascal was smiling at some private plan you didn't want to know about.

"This is it, I guess," Di was saying, as she and Tom found a seat near the back of the bus. "I mean here's phase one, like we're pretty much over this part, that whole part leading up to the bus part." She was twirling her wrist frantically and had been doing so half the night, awake, feeling the dread eat her up from the insides, like a snake was loose in there. She'd dreamt about a skull too, with huge empty eyes and this collapsed smile. "Dreams are just plain twisted, I swear," she said. "Tom, did I tell you about this skull I saw. Tom?"

Tom had not slept much, either. He had been up on his roof again, staring into the darkness over the ocean. He had had what he called his eye-in-the-sky vision, where he would feel the tingling in his lower back and then—*sproing!*—he would see himself from above, like he was looking down from a plane. He'd seen everything from up high: the roofs of Adjacent, the Point, the plant, Mount Trashmore. Now as he took his seat he seemed to be shrinking again.

"Look," Di said. "If that annoying Ham can survive, so can we. Right? Did you see his nose hairs? They got longer, seriously longer. They're curly, like his hair, and there's crumbs in them, like from his toast or something. It's disgusting, if you ask me."

She sensed a faint smile from beneath the Angels cap.

In minutes they had crossed the causeway, the narrow bridge to Crotona, and the bus turned right, passed a grimy strip mall with wig shops and a liquor store, and chugged up a hill, on a twisting road that dead-ended into the school parking lot.

This is it, thought Di. Her wrist circled in her lap. The schoolyard was a seething swarm of buses, teachers, school security, and students. Kids of all ages, some chasing each other, others hugging like long-lost family, or pushing each other in fake fights, posing, slouching. Some were sitting in circles on the concrete, with their backpacks and hats and sunglasses and braided bracelets and colored hair and whatever. Tom stared bug-eyed out the bus window. This was a real school, as big and sprawling and busy as a miniature city; you could drop Adjacent Elementry in the corner of the yard and no one would even notice it was there.

"You know, one thing is, maybe we should kinda stay near the door?" Di said. "You could maybe get lost out there. That's my theory on this whole situation. My working theory."

TriCounty was a fortress of smudged yellow brick. The main building had a giant clock tower and behind it were four huge cinderblock cells, three stories each, surrounding a tiny courtyard. Beneath a gray archway stood two massive wooden dungeon doors: the entrance.

Di felt a glare coming from one knot of Crotona kids. She studied them out of the corner of her eye: older, most of them, boys and some girls. They were looking over at the Adjacent group, all right, smiling in a miserable way.

"Make way for islanders!" one of them yelled, a tall, athletic boy with a patch of chin hair and a head of long, curly hair.

"Tribal peoples," said another.

"Oot-landers!"

They weren't even in the building yet and things were getting dicey, Di thought. What next?

When the bell finally rang, the herd of students—some the size of grown adults—surged through the giant doors, carrying

Di and Tom into what could have been the inside of a huge, diseased lung.

Brown everywhere. Brown walls, brown classroom doors, rows of light-brown lockers. Yellow-brown ceilings with peeling paint like the underside of a rusting car.

The river of bodies poured into the brown maze of hallways, nearly crawling over one another, each one somehow knowing exactly where to go. Several security guards and hall monitors circled the entranceway, and one of them rounded up Di, Tom, and a few other kids who had the same homeroom, Mrs. Turboff's room.

Mrs. Turboff, a social studies teacher, stood at the door like a commanding officer, a short older lady with a hatchet face, wearing one of those deep frowns that is a smile underneath.

"Welcome!" Mrs. Turboff said, loudly, once everyone was seated. "Now, I'd like each of you to say your name and something else about yourself if you like. But you don't have to, if you'd rather not." When everyone had spoken (some, like Tom, so softly that no one heard them), Mrs. Turboff told them about their first day.

They would spend only fifteen minutes in each class, meet their teachers, get their books, find their lockers, and that was about all. And she told them to consider this class their home base.

"Any problems, any trouble finding a class, you come back here and see me. OK?"

Good, Di thought. OK so far.

A loud insect-like buzzing filled the air and then a strange voice came over the PA system.

"Greetings, students, this is Principal Zommocco. Time to move to your next class. Now, please. New students, if you don't know where to go, learn. You're here to learn after all."

A slow, lazy voice, Di thought. Half awake, and not kind. The only class that Di and Tom had together, it turned out, was math. Third period, Mr. Williams.

Mr. Williams wore a bowtie and had a pointed chin and nose and long, gray-black hair slicked back and greasy.

The first thing that Di noticed about him was he had yellowish teeth with a kind of brown stripe at the bottom. His eyes were huge. One was normal, but the other one kind of bobbed and floated around. You couldn't tell if he was checking on people with that roving eye or if it had just come unhooked from the socket.

"Greetings to you, young masters," Mr. Williams said. He settled the class and told them that they would be learning a lot that semester. How to factor numbers. How to calculate the areas of surfaces and volumes. To use the x-axis and y-axis.

He drew those axes on the board, along with some other shapes and figures, and put in some coordinates. At one point he turned from the board, marched to the center of the class, and started staring at something on the back wall—no one knew what. He stood there and stared, as still as a statue, in a trance, a full-blown, bug-eyed trance. Di and Tom looked at each other; they had no idea what to think.

The Adjacent grapevine was mixed on Mr. Williams. Some said he was a twisted freak with a gargoyle eye, and others said he was really good if you tried, even if you didn't know jack about math.

"All right," he said—and here he held up an index finger high in the air and raised his voice—"but know this. In this class you will solve problems. Easy ones at first and harder ones later, more than you want perhaps."

He stopped, and his eyes widened again. "And I do not want to hear anyone say—ever—that he or she will not use these skills in real life. Oh yes you will, if you want to stay sane. Yes you will, or your brain will gorge on itself. Eat itself alive. That's the only way I stay sane, and barely. Do you understand?"

The entire class nodded its head in unison. No one had any idea what he was talking about. Again came the electronic insect whine of the PA: *"Next class, student body. Move, now. The room numbers are right there on the schedules you should have from your homeroom."*

Mr. Williams glanced up at the speaker, annoyed.

"OK then. Please take a book from the stack on your way out. Be prepared to begin solving problems by tomorrow, and not to stop until June."

A few of the kids pulled a bug-eyed Williams stare before they were even out of the room. Tom picked up his book and nearly stumbled he was so eager to get out; Di followed, and saw Tom on one knee in the hallway, trying to find something on right triangles. She had almost forgotten in the anxious rush of the day that they had other problems to solve, and a missing person to find.

They found a paragraph on the right triangle rule in the book, and a name for the triangle rule. There it was: The Pythagorean theorem, it was called, after some guy, Pythagoras, who was the leader of a secret cult of people who studied numbers. Kids had drawn so many different mustaches, glasses, and sideburns on their books' pictures of Pythagoras that his face was invisible. Di imagined a young man with dark hair, whispering in some secret number language to his friends.

"He would know about the triangle, and maybe could help us with the other numbers," Tom said.

"Pythagoras? No way he's still alive."

"No, Di, stop being a clown. Him"—he nodded toward Mr. Williams's door.

They picked up their books and stepped toward the door and found when they got there that they didn't have the nerve to go in.

The rest of the day went quickly, and soon Di was back out in the yard again, looking for the black, beat-up Adjacent bus. That's where she saw the knot of kids again, the ones who had yelled at them that morning. Di noticed one of them in particular, tall with long curly hair, with a patch of chin hair and what looked like something dripping on his cheek. He was by far the best-looking boy she'd ever seen.

"That's Virgil," a girl from English class whispered to her. "Owen Wilfred. He's insane. Makes everyone call him Virgil. No one calls him by his real name. He's the leader of the Poets."

"What's wrong with his cheek?" Di asked.

"Teardrop tattoos. Seriously. Some kids call him Teardrop but you better not let the Poets hear that."

"Huh?" Di said. "Poets? You got to be kidding."

"The Epic Poets. That's the main Crotona gang. See, they've got those earrings, and that soul patch thing on their chins. If they can't grow it on, they put it on with a marker." The girl frowned and moved away.

Di moved toward the group more closely and saw that it was true, some of them had colored in their patch in marker. She moved in closer, trying not to giggle: the Poets!

"Hey, fat ass, what you laughing at?" someone hissed at her, and she snorted in a half-laugh, half-scream and her gum shot out of her mouth at the curly-haired Virgil guy. She saw the older boy's thick lips recoil in a smile of pure disgust.

"What the living—" someone said.

She snagged her backpack and ran, leaped into the bus, and collapsed beside Tom, breathless.

"Gawd. Did you see that? What did I freaking do?" she said. "Oh, I am the worst. Did you see them, Tom? That big one's called, uh"—she lowered her voice way down—"the Virgil, and he's got teardrop tattoos, that's why he looks so scary, and that's a Crotona gang, they're called the Epic Poets, and oh, brother, can you believe it?"

Tom didn't answer.

"Tom. Ground control to Major Tom—"

"I know what the numbers mean," he said. "And I know what we need to do."

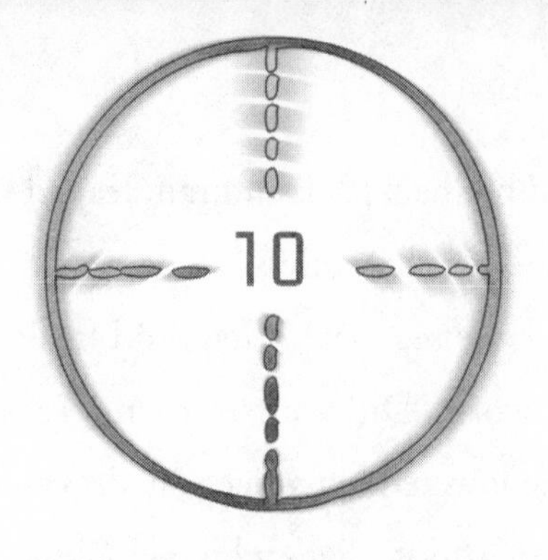

MAPMAKING

TOM'S SOLUTION WAS SIMPLE. IT SEEMED TO HIM TOO easy, in fact, like elementary school math. Yet it had the right feeling, and it made every other idea he had look limp by comparison. But first things first; the two of them had to check in with his dad, who had a food cart near the plant, serving kebab wrap sandwiches. Tom's dad had agreed with Mrs. Smith that he would keep track of the kids this afternoon.

"You take this and go back close to the house," he told them, handing out two warm kebabs dripping with sauces. "Tell your sister you are there, and just stay close, understand."

The kebab wraps lasted less than a minute. Di and Tom sat there, on plastic chairs behind Tom's trailer, and both had the same thought: This afternoon would have been the most precious Mrs. Clarke time of all.

She would have listened to everything, about the swarming schoolyard and Mrs. Turboff. About the rotting intestines of TriCounty, how the light seemed to turn brown in there. She would have smiled about Mr. Williams and his wide, wobbly eyes. Those two knew one another, Di remembered. Mrs. Clarke also would have tried to ease Di's worries about the Poets.

"OK," Tom said, pulling out a pencil and a used envelope. "Here's what I think. Take a look at this map. This circle is the island, and here's Adjacent."

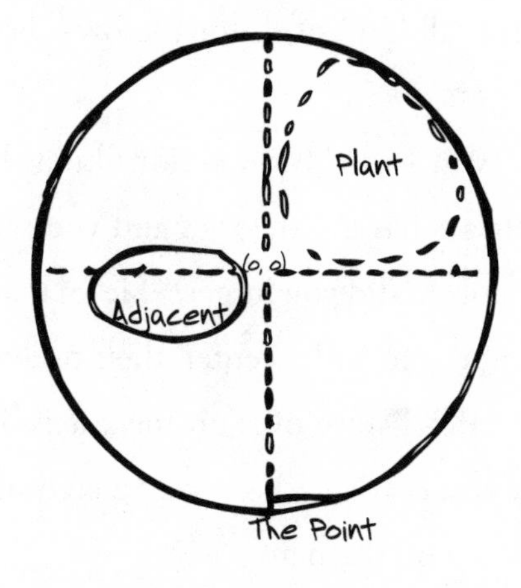

"You see where these two lines cross in the middle?" Tom said.

Di nodded. "Yeah, OK, of course. So what?"

"Well, remember those two pipes we found, in that room under the outhouses? That was right about the middle of the island—look at the map—and those two pipes crossed each other exactly like this."

“I remember, yeah, I was there. So what?”

“So today, in Mr. Williams’s class, when he drew that graph thing with the x-axis and y-axis, did you see? The point at the middle was zero zero—just like on the pipes. I mean, not just on the pipes, but right exactly where they crossed. That’s where it was written. On purpose.”

Di stared at the map for a few moments more.

“So you mean these underground pipes are the island’s x-axis and y-axis? But then what do the other numbers mean, twelve and eight? This is all kind of, I don’t know—how do we know any of this is right?”

“We don’t,” said Tom. “But we didn’t know last time. You’re the one who always has the theories and you said we had to at least try it last time, or did you forget?” He let that sink in. “Look at the map. If zero zero is the center, then twelve eight must be another point, OK? Twelve over on the x-axis line, either right or left. Positive or negative. Then you go eight up on the y-axis line.” He drew this on the map:

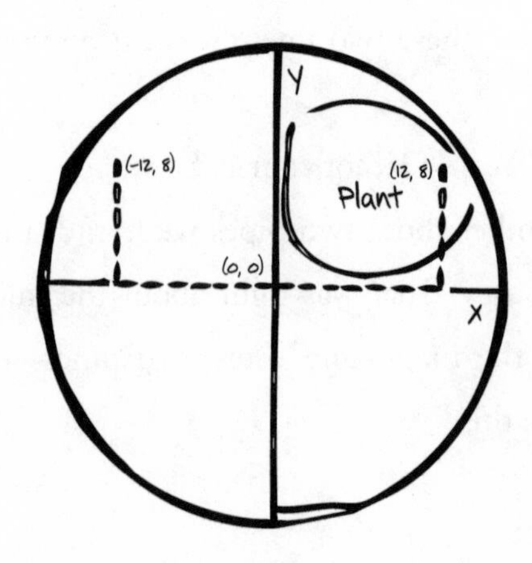

"But twelve what?" Di said. "Oh, right. Twelve hundred yards, like we did last time. I say let's—" She didn't finish. Tom was up on his feet and she hustled to catch up.

He was faster but she had an instinct for picking the best route through the trailers and yards. By the time they were clear of the trailers, Di was out ahead with Tom closing fast.

As they scrambled past the trailers, she blocked him, held him by the shirt, and knocked him over several times on the way, using her superior size. Tom weaved back and forth, pushing back and having seizures of silent laughter.

They were so out of breath when they got to the outhouses that they fell onto the gravel and lay there on their backs until they could stop laughing and breathe again.

"You gotta stop falling down," Di spat out between breaths. "Maybe you'd win a race once in the next billion years if you didn't keep wiping out. You need your legs checked."

"As soon as you get your butt checked—" That's when Tom noticed something, something in the ground. A row of faint divots in the rocky soil, every twenty yards or so, that extended outward from the outhouses. He got up and examined one of the divots closely, dug into the soil for about a foot, and hit something hard. It was steel. He dug around it some more and found a rod with its tip painted bright red.

"Hey, Di. Look at this." He walked around the outhouses. Sure enough, he saw lines of the divots—indentations the size of a football, really. The divots ran off from the outhouse directly north, south, east, and west:

"What are they?"

"Maybe that's so they know where the pipe is, if they have to fix it?" Tom said. "Like if you have to dig down and find it. Or maybe where two pieces join together, you know?"

"Yeah, maybe," she said. "But who cares? It gives us a path, right? The x- and y-axes are marked for us."

They followed this trail as best they could for twelve hundred yards due east, away from Adjacent and toward the plant. This was the plus side of the x-axis, on the map. The pacing led them near the plant fence, on their left, and not far from the edge of the island.

"Not good," Di said.

To their right was a wasteland they had played in a thousand times; no secret tunnels there. To their left was the ten-foot-tall chain-link fence with barbed wire on top—possible, for a skilled climber, but perfectly insane. Guard hounds roamed in there, and no one had the least interest in getting trapped inside.

"Oh, brother," said Di. She was rotating her wrist. "This is it? No way we're going in there. I hate that place. Forget this. I'm not going to get shriveled by radioactive gas or whatever they have in there. Mutant hounds. Or mines. Army mines, I heard they have those, they blow off a leg but you're still alive."

Tom put up a hand for her to stop. "OK, OK. No, of course we're not going in there," he said. "Impossible with all that security anyway."

They stood for a while outside the fence, in the long shadows of late afternoon, and to Di the island seemed suddenly emptier and lonelier than ever.

"Give me that map," Di said finally. "I'm going to do what Mrs. Clarke always said: try anything, try every stupid thing."

Tom straightened up. "Hold on. Let's see that again, the map—" he said.

"No, don't grab it!" Di said. "I'm looking at it. Let me look at it. You're the one who brought us out here to the middle of nuclear nowhere. Why don't we—let's go twelve hundred yards in the other direction. Toward Adjacent from the outhouse. It looked like there was a negative sign in front of the twelve anyway. At least it's something to do. I don't want to stand around here anymore. I hate it here. Let's at least pretend there's a solution and pretend we're not too stupid to find it, OK?"

Tom cracked up. Another Mrs. Clarke line: When the going got desperate, pretend there's a solution and that you're going to find it. Yeah, that worked every time. They tracked the pipe back to Adjacent, counting paces. The line of divots disappeared under the trailers but the line by then was pretty clear and ran parallel to the plant road. The walk took them past the center of town, past DeepEnd, Polya's, and the Bamboo, toward an area of the island near the edge called Far Corner.

FC was the sketchiest part of Adjacent, out toward the garbage dump, with people living in sheds, hounds on chains, abandoned cars, burned-out trailers. Di and Tom, like every other sane human, stayed way clear of Far Corner.

As they approached that ragged cluster of trailers and sheds, the barking started. First a shrill chirping from a small hound, and then a chorus of a half dozen hounds. Two pit bulls, both on short chains, were going crazy, running in circles. At least two other hounds were now coming toward them, slowly, like wolves.

"Oh brother, this is nuts. We're going to get eaten any second here," Di said.

They stopped, unsure whether to turn and walk. Or run.

And then the barking went quiet. The approaching hounds—German shepherds, Di saw—held their places, staring.

A small boy had appeared at the edge of the clutch of trailers, and comforted one of the pit bulls. The boy was dark and small with huge eyes and he turned an open palm toward them, about chest-high—was he waving? It was hard for them to tell.

"That's that boy who came to Mrs. Clarke's a couple of times. Remember?"

"Yeah. Oki Something. Homeschooled. He lives out here?" They waited until the two German shepherds turned away, before continuing along the road. The twelve hundred mark was not far from the edge of the cliffs on the negative arm of the x-axis.

"Jeez, thanks, Mrs. Clarke. First we're under an outhouse, and now we're in FC. What's next?" Di said.

"That is," Tom said, pointing to the right, where Mount Trashmore loomed brown and seething in the silver afternoon light. The wind shifted and the smell immediately hit them, a tangy, chemical swamp reek.

"Aagh, I can't even look," said Di. "This is worse than the plant. I'm sorry. I thought I had an idea. It's so much easier when you're just working these things out on paper, you don't have to walk through nuclear gas and giant crud piles, you know?"

Tom was staring at the ground, with a forearm over his nose, and began to walk back toward Adjacent. Di stayed put.

"Tom? Hold up," she said. "What was it the security guy said, about the caves and the dump? And Mr. Pink, like, got mad at him?"

They stood there in the road for a while, thinking.

"You know what, and I hate myself for saying this, but I'm going to anyway. We should go talk to Ham. Ham will have an idea. He's the one person we know who could help."

Tom stared at her. He could imagine nothing worse than having to speak to Hamilton Rowan, the kid who'd lost his mind under Mount Trashmore for no reason. Everyone knows at least one kid who loses his head and can't get it back. Someone who was hilarious or smart or good in sports or all three, and then something happened and it all changed. It was just—over.

Before his Trashmore stunt, Ham was one of those kids who's constantly pulling pranks and thinking they're all funny, no matter how stupid. Whether he loosened the wheels on your bike or dropped a lizard into your backpack or spiked your cream soda with laxative or vodka, he laughed insanely. He'd scam anybody too, even Rene D., Pascal, and friends. That got him beaten badly several times, and it was almost like he enjoyed it. He had been a dangerous lunatic, when you really thought about it.

Not anymore. Now he did nothing but lie around for hours behind his parents' trailer, with a book on his lap, like he was reading.

He wasn't; he would just nap, and once in a while kind of nod, as if agreeing with someone. Or whittle, with his huge hunting knife. Tom would not go near him, under any circumstances. Di knew better than to approach him in school. Ham was in ninth grade, and if anyone saw them even talking it would get around either that Ham was getting more pathetic or that Di was becoming some kind of village-idiot mental patient, like he was.

So she waited for the weekend, and still tried to talk herself out of approaching him. But in the end it had to be done. Whatever was happening, it had something to do with tunnels and the plant. Mr. Romo, Mrs. Quartez, and clearly Mrs. Clarke too had all known about the caves.

"We're going, and you're coming with me," Di said to Tom on that Saturday morning.

Ham Rowan was parked on a plastic lounger, as usual. It looked like he had just finished breakfast. His hair had grown long, Di noticed, and he'd also gained weight. He looked almost like a bum, like a man, like he could be another Big Sip in training. He had some kind of brown stuff at the corners of his mouth; Di wished he would wipe it off.

"Ham?" His head tipped slightly but his eyes didn't find Di. "Ham?" she said again. No response. "Ham!"

Now he stared in her direction, with impassive, dumb eyes.

"Ham, can I ask you something?" A ghost of a smile ran across his lips, and he looked away again.

Di watched him for a moment, wondering what was going on in his head. If anything. He had that floating look. She didn't know what to say next so she went right to the point.

"Ham, I want to go into the tunnels under Trashmore. I know they're down there." Which she didn't; she was guessing.

Again, nothing. Ham picked up the book that was lying on his knees—it was called *Delta Force*, Di saw—and pretended to read, then put it down and stared up into the sky.

"Oh brother, this stinks, why don't bigger kids ever listen to what people say? Ham, please. Remember that one time we hid in the luggage rack of the—"

"I miss it," he said. He was still staring away and Di saw his lips tighten. "That, all that. Yeah, we were up in that luggage rack and Rene D. and them clowns were looking in the bus, walked right past us. You were, like, three years old. I miss how it was back then."

"I was seven."

Ham turned and looked at Di for the first time, studying her face as if to make sure she was the same person he'd hidden with. "Why do you want to go down into the tunnels?"

Di shot a sideways look at Tom. They hadn't even known for sure there were tunnels down there.

"Because we have to. Because that's the only way we can save our friend, Mrs. Clarke. Because we miss her. Because something bad's happening in Adjacent. To Adjacent. I mean, everyone's either at the Bamboo or working all the time, like my mom, and no one's noticing."

Ham reached for the Delta Force book again, found a page near the beginning, and seemed to read it carefully. He was concentrating hard, and sort of speaking the words to himself. Di knew that English wasn't Ham's strong suit and wondered for a moment whether he could read at all. She was pretty sure his parents couldn't.

"Ham? If you don't—"

"OK," he said, closing the book and looking up. "I'll show you how to get down there, is all."

It was late morning, and Di and Tom were dying for a snack and a break, but they could not afford to lose Ham. Di followed him, a few paces back, and Tom trailed at a distance. They weaved through neighboring trailers, ducked under several, went up and over one, then slipped through a hole in a fence and were out on the main road, where they turned left.

Ham and Di left the road near FC and angled off toward Trashmore. Tom let them go ahead. He moved off the road as well, but stopped to scour the ground, looking for the trail of the underground pipe, their x-axis. He found the divots, relocated the marker they had left at twelve hundred yards, and began to count toward the mountain. He wanted to be sure. He had no confidence in Ham. When Tom arrived he saw Di and Ham picking through garbage, some fifty yards away. It was a good thing he had carefully mapped the location. The other two were wandering, a few hundred yards off the point Tom had mapped.

"Hey!" Tom yelled. He waved his arms and pointed at the location. By his calculation, (-12, 8) was less than a hundred yards straight ahead of where he was standing, directly under the mountain.

Di came running up, and Ham followed, out of breath. The geezer really was getting bulky, that was for sure, Tom thought.

"It's right back in there," said Di, pointing with Tom.

"What? How do you know?" said Ham.

"We just do. We do. Can't we just find it? I mean, is there really something in there? You just said you were looking for the entrance, so maybe it's right in here somewhere."

"Right, get outta my way," he said. Ham kicked his way toward the bottom of the hill, through a shambles of trash bags, broken furniture, old TVs, and skateboard sneakers. Food everywhere. Soggy bread, chicken bones, black squashed bananas, and meat crawling with insects. An entire rotting universe, reeking like sugary vomit.

Ham was looking for something, and Di wanted to scream for him to hurry his freaking self up.

Finally, his black jeans crusty with junk, Ham made his way to a pair of old refrigerators brown and rotting and leaning against one another, barely visible in the walls of garbage. He slipped between the two fridges and disappeared.

"Oh brother, what's he doing?" Di said after several minutes. "He's not getting lost again, is he?"

"Clam it, clown!" Ham yelled back, from somewhere behind the fridges. "This is it. Follow me."

They crept forward, trying to ignore the squishy mess underfoot. On the other side of the refrigerators was a sticky corridor that ran under the hill. Speckles of light somehow drifted through the junk. Di and Tom followed Ham for exactly sixty-three yards—Tom counted every pace—and they arrived at (-12, 8). This had to be it. Ham had stopped and he was pointing down at the ground.

And there it was: another hole in the ground, like the one under the outhouse, with a ladder descending.

"OK," Ham said. "I'm, uh, I'm going to take a break before going down there. But here you are."

The tremor in his voice made both Di and Tom take a breath. Tom had a sense that they were already deep into something bad—literally, under a mountain of junk—and he figured that at least the hole would not smell so bad. He went down first. He got to the bottom of the hole quickly and saw nothing. Complete blackness. Di followed and crouched there at the bottom of the ladder for a time.

The smell was worse; it was now a stinging ammonia reek,

and the light was a ghostly black-gray blindfold that they could not blink away. The stillness, the cool humming silence seemed to seep in through their skin. Their eyes adjusted only enough to estimate the outlines of the place. Circular, like the other one, and man-made, larger than a living room. Openings in the walls—tunnels?—that seemed to head off in a dozen different directions.

Ham joined them after a while and seemed to freeze in place. Di groped to locate him and found that he was trembling, badly. It was down here, not digging in the garbage, where Ham lost his way, Di was now certain.

She, like Tom, was straining her eyes to find another clue, anything really, that would give them a reason to climb out. It was Ham who saw it.

"Hey, check this out," he said. He was pointing up at the ceiling of the craggy room. And there it was: a series of numbers, scrawled in chalk. Again, Mrs. Clarke's handwriting:

$$m = -4, m = 1/5 \text{ @ } (-8, -8)$$

Tom stood on his tiptoes to study it, to be sure. He looked down at Di, eyes wide.

"I can't believe this," she said. Di could not imagine Mrs. Clarke somehow making her way down here, into this underground hovel; not in a million years. Not ever. In that moment it occurred to her dimly that maybe there was more to Mrs. Clarke than she had thought. The woman had been in the Navy, married to that SEAL for a while. And she had clearly climbed underneath an outhouse to leave the last clue. "Unbelievable," she said. "I mean, it's happening. It's real. These are clues and we found them. We did it. We did it again. Didn't we? Oh brother, what we need is an answer key, like in the back of a textbook, that tells you how to get the answers, you know? But it sure looks like we did it, huh Tom?"

"Did what?" Ham said. "You're a long way from the plant. I assume that's where you want to go, cuz there's no other reason to be crawling around down here. I'm sure not going any farther unless someone gives me a map through this maze. Now, can we get out of here?"

Di and Tom looked at each other: The tunnels led to the plant?

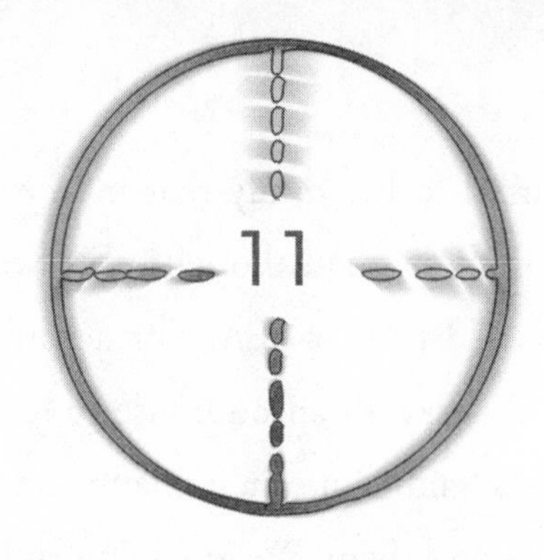

THE SILVER COMPASS

DI AWOKE LATE THE NEXT MORNING, AFRAID. SHE HAD had nightmares, of being buried alive, of feeling wet, white worms nibbling at her skin. The smiling skull with hollow eyes was back too, and this time it was trying to tell her something, she thought.

By the time she sat up in bed her mom was awake and gone, probably shopping or having coffee with friends. That was a relief. Di didn't want to be quizzed by her mother, not until she had some idea of what was really going on. She made an English muffin with peanut butter, poured herself a glass of milk, and tried to relax for a few minutes.

Her stomach wouldn't let her. The shadow of the night's visions still lingered, and she felt a strange stirring when she stepped outside and sat on the steps. What was it? A Sunday in

September, warm, and everything looked the same as always. People were out, playing cards, gossiping, or sitting on their stoops, drinking iced tea or beer. Several radios were on too loud, one blaring a county-and-western station, another pounding hip-hop.

She walked toward Polya's and noticed a feeling of urgency or expectation—an alien sensation for Adjacent, where people never expected anything to happen. Di noticed little things. Mr. Devlin, Mr. Paulos, and a few others were sitting on a tire, sipping beer; an early start even for them, and they were unusually subdued.

Others milled around there as well, many more than usual; the Bamboo was almost full of drinkers. It felt like some kind of special occasion—a bad one, like a funeral.

"Lady Di, love, you be careful now," Mrs. Polya said when Di paid for a pair of cream sodas. Mrs. Polya was kind of like a mother for the whole island, when you thought about it. She was like that even before her son died way back, people said. Not that any kids really remembered him; he was "not all there" and out of high school when he fell or jumped from the cliffs out by the plant, was the story. Mr. Polya left the island not long after that, and if you stood still long enough some adult would lecture you about how everything changed when Georgie Polya was lost. Ancient history, really.

"They got two security men in town now," Mrs. Polya was

saying, "and I assume you know what's going on. They're looking for something. They're going through people's homes now. Mrs. Penfield came in here and said they went through her drawers, all of them. They even searched under her trailer. You and your friend might want to think about whether you want to go back home now or later."

Di glanced back at Tom, who had materialized behind her. One look told her that he was thinking the same thing: Mr. Pink hadn't said so directly but had given them both the impression that he was looking for something Mrs. Clarke had. Plant security must have decided that it was time to stop asking and start searching.

Di could not face another interrogation, not now, not after having gotten in this deep, and literally still smelling faintly of Trashmore. Ditto for Tom. Both were sore, after the crouching and crawling of the day before, and wanted nothing more than to sip a cold cream soda, maybe watch some TV. It wasn't going to happen. Di groaned deeply.

"We need to find out what happened to Ham down there," she said to Tom as they left the store. "Oh brother, and we can't take too much time solving this clue. Maybe Ham can help us. I know he's not exactly great at school or anything, but he's in high school math."

They found him in the same place as before, draped over a lounge chair in back of his place, asleep. Mr. Rowan was back there too, playing cards with friends around a small table. Di stifled another groan. Mr. Rowan was barefoot, sunburned, his belly spilling out of a tight T-shirt that said PROMISING GRADUATE STUDENT on it. A giant bottle of whiskey sat in the middle of the table, wreathed in cigarette smoke. Di and Tom slipped into the yard without attracting the attention of the men. They crept up beside Ham and tapped him on the shoulder. His eyes opened immediately.

"What?" he said. Instantly awake, almost like he was waiting for them.

"Ham, we need to talk to you again. Please," said Di. "Can we, can you, could we go away from here, where we could talk without adults around, OK?"

Ham took a while to budge but finally did. It was strange, thought Di. He had been so wild before, always in motion, and now he was like a big, old hound, too spent to do anything but lift its head (and a good thing, she thought, otherwise there was no way they would have been able find him, much less learn anything from him). In minutes they were safely hidden in the bus graveyard, in Di and Tom's luxury liner. Di could tell that Ham had not been in this bus before.

"So this is your conference room?" Ham said. "Who will be giving their PowerPoint presentation first?"

"You will," said Di. "Listen, do you see what's happening, even sort of? Mrs. Clarke was taken away and people are disappearing and now everyone's being searched. And Ham, Tom and I are trying to do something,"

"Tom who?" He looked around. "You mean Jones?"

They told him everything. Tom pulled out one of the maps he had drawn to make it all clear. He now carried an updated version folded up in his back pocket. Ham's face, with that little tuft of blondish hair on his limp mouth that was supposed to be facial hair, showed no evidence of interest. He was listening, though, because he was nodding almost imperceptibly as Di spoke.

"Now, you tell us," Di said. "What happened in the tunnels? What happened to you down there?" She couldn't quite believe she was talking to Hamilton Rowan this way. He didn't seem to mind, though. Maybe that's what happened when you lost your head, your energy, your life force: Nothing much mattered anymore. He stared at his hands for a while, looked away, and shook his head.

"I got lost," he said, in a small voice. He shook his head again, more slowly, staring at the floor. "Lost. There are so many tunnels down there. You think you can find your way back, but I learned that if you don't leave markers and you turn the wrong way . . ." He took the pen and the map. "Here's what I can tell you about the tunnels, the ones I know about. And the ones I know go nowhere. It kinda looks like this."

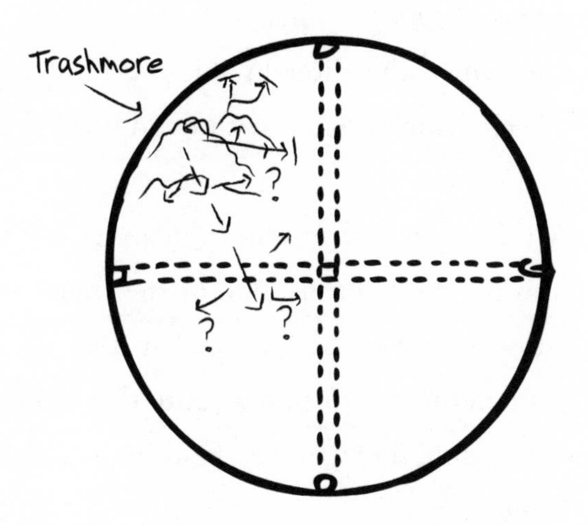

In fragments, broken by that faraway look, he told them more, much more. The tunnels off the room under the Trashmore entrance were almost all man-made corridors, narrow and craggy but also straight and meant for an adult to walk through. Ham said that the tunnels hadn't been used in years, that they were crumbling and cracked and dangerous in places, so badly you weren't sure what was a tunnel and what was just cracked rock.

Some were blocked entirely, caved in and impassible. You had to have a flashlight, he said, plus a backup flashlight and ideally a helmet, or something to make sure you didn't get knocked out. You were constantly banging your head down there. In some parts, too, you had to lie down on your stomach and push through like a snake, wondering if you would get stuck for good.

"Stuck and no one knows where—"

His head jerked at the thought, his eye blinked: that new tic he had. He hadn't done it with them until then, Di noticed.

He said that the tunnels that went from under Trashmore back inland toward the Crotona side of the island were a mess, mostly caved in. He had explored in that direction because he was determined to find a route that went under Trashmore, so he could emerge and claim he had tunneled all the way through.

"But that's all jammed up over on that side. You can't get through," he said. "And this big pipe, the x-axis pipe, is pretty ruined, and totally blocked right about here"—he pointed to a spot about five hundred yards from (0, 0).

He shook his head and looked up. "And there's this thunder down there. I think it's coming from the plant. It's so freaking loud. Animals and insects and stuff go running wild."

Di nodded at him, eyes wide. Tom had turned away, and seemed to be shrinking into himself again.

Di forced herself to think about the new clue, to steer her mind from the thunder. "That's what the numbers are for, Ham, to guide us through," she said.

Tom had written them down on the back of the map:

$$m = -4,\ m = 1/5 \ @ \ (-8, -8)$$

He handed it to Ham.

Ham didn't seem to look at it at all. He was staring away again, up somewhere in the middle of the bus ceiling. Tom watched him as if the older boy were an escaped zoo animal. What would it do next? Was it, in fact, thinking? He hoped so. Once people start thinking, as Mrs. Clarke would have said, all bets are off. You have no idea what they can do, and neither do they. Ham said: "I don't know. I'm not exactly a genius, you know what I'm saying. But look. The *m*, I mean, it could be the slope. You know, the slope of a line? You heard of it, right?"

No answer.

"You haven't. You're kidding, right?"

"No, we haven't," Di said. "We're in seventh grade, Ham, not high school, OK? From the top-rated Adjacent Elementry math program, have you heard of that? Are you going to tell us or not?"

He explained that the slope in math is a lot like the slope of a hill. It's a measure of steepness. A slope of 5 is steeper than a slope of 1; a slope of 1 is steeper than a slope of ½. The closer you get to 0, the closer you get to level ground: no steepness.

He took a piece of paper from Tom and drew some lines.

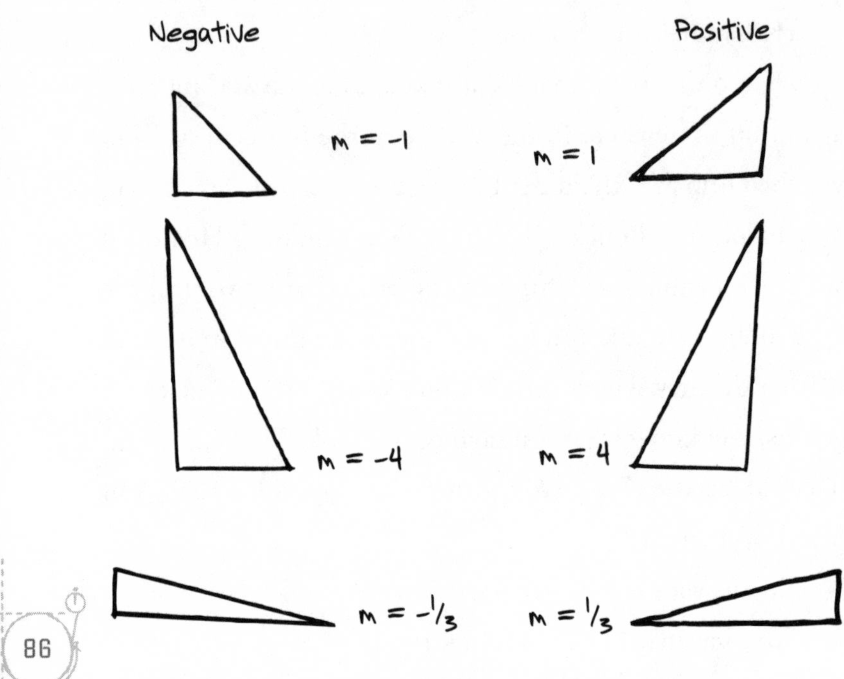

"See," Ham said. "Easy."

Di glanced up at Tom, who was perched on a seat.

"Yeah, sure. Easy," she said. She wasn't sure why she was so annoyed. She thought maybe it was the way some people explained stuff they already knew as if everyone else already knew it. "Uh, but Ham, one thing. How do you actually get the number for the slope? What does 'm equals negative four' actually mean?"

"Oh," Ham said. "Right. But you already know how to do that. It's exactly what you've been doing, using a right triangle. The slope is just the distance you move up or down on the y-axis divided by the number you move along to one side, to get to another point on the line," he said. "That's all it is."

He shrugged. "So it looks to me for instance like you could have only one line going through this spot under Trashmore, with a slope of four. Er, I guess that's a minus sign. Negative four. So it would look like this. See, you're just using the right triangle again. You can use that for a ton of stuff."

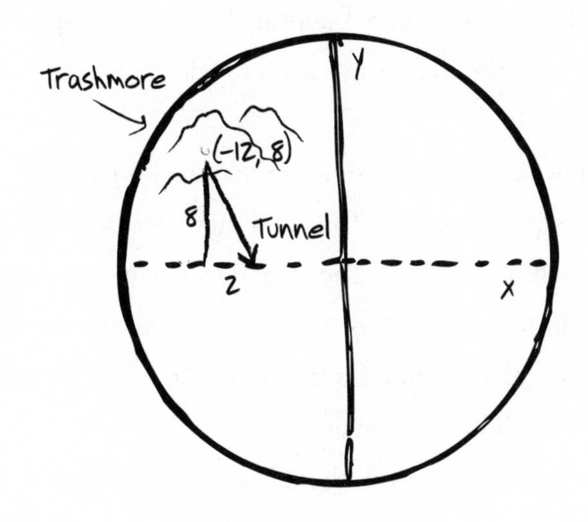

They stared at the drawing.

"That line should go right to the big x-pipe, right into it," Di said.

"'Zactly. 'Zactly right," said Ham. "The tunnels are straight, and that one should go right to the big pipe. You got a case of the 'zactlies." He picked up the paper and drew the line. In one direction it went up toward Crotona and hit a dead end at the edge of the island. In the other direction the line hit the pipe that they called the x-axis.

They plotted it out exactly and found that the line—the tunnel—moved four hundred yards along the y-axis for every one hundred yards it moved along the x-axis.

They drew this line on their map, as it moved out from under Trashmore. The tunnel appeared to hit the x-pipe at a point about one thousand yards from the dead-center point on the island, (0, 0).

"But how do you know for sure the tunnel is straight?"

The question came from Tom, and they were the first words ever between him and Ham. The older boy kind of shifted in his chair without looking directly at Tom. That was the way older kids were around Tom Jones: If they weren't hunting him down it was like they didn't see him at all.

His question was critical, though. Without an answer they could get just as lost as Ham had. How can you possibly know where you're going, in the dark, down there? Ham sat up and dug deep into a front pocket. He was wearing shorts that came down almost to his ankles, with huge pockets. He pulled out a handful of stuff: a yo-yo, nail clippers, marbles, a snake skull, his hunting knife, some wadded up papers, his Delta Force book, and a compass.

"I been thinking about this for a while," he said. "I never had a line to follow down there at first, no way to know which way I was going." He held up the compass. "You should be able to use this. First find north, by lining up the needle with the letter N. Then, point the thing straight down the tunnel, to find out if it's the tunnel you want. And as long as the needle points in the same direction as you move, you're going straight." He pulled out the diagram and used the compass on the page.

"Observe," Ham said. It read 14 degrees. "You just point the compass the way you're going and make sure it stays on fourteen degrees away from south."

"That's it?"

"That's it." Then he stared at them. "That and your brain. You got to be able to turn your brain off down there. Blank. Nothing. If you can't do that, you won't get back out."

THUNDER UNDERGROUND

ON TV YOU SEE PEOPLE HAVING MEETINGS IN OFFICES ALL the time, talking about strategy, giving presentations or whatever. They usually look pretty slick and have stacks of papers and talk about "clients" and whatnot, and you have to ask, Who are these people, exactly? Are they for real? Where do people like that live?

Not in Adjacent, is where.

No one ever had a planning meeting for anything here. Maybe once, when Rene D. and Pascal organized a team of kids to pull one of the old buses from the graveyard, roll it out to the cliffs, and push it over. Sucker rolled over the edge in slow motion, sort of, and did this flip and hit the rocks like an A-bomb. Broken glass everywhere. That was one of the best days ever.

It just wasn't the sort of organizing that gave Di confidence that her plan, with Tom and Ham, would work. She wasn't even sure that they had guessed the meaning of the *m*'s correctly, and it could all go wrong underground; she could tell from just listening to Ham that things were twisted down there.

But it was all they had and a simple enough idea. Find the tunnel that went from the Trashmore entrance back toward the x-pipe at a slope of minus four. Only one tunnel could fit that description.

Then—the clue seemed to suggest—proceed to the point (-8, -8), where the tunnel with the slope of $\frac{1}{5}$ intersected the minus-four-slope one. Turn left, and get to the y-pipe. If they could. Exploring, that's all they were doing, Di told herself.

The compass needle would always point north, toward Crotona, Ham reminded them as they headed back out to Trashmore. So if you rotated the compass to point down the line of the tunnel, the needle would appear to be 166 degrees off of north and 14 degrees away from dead south.

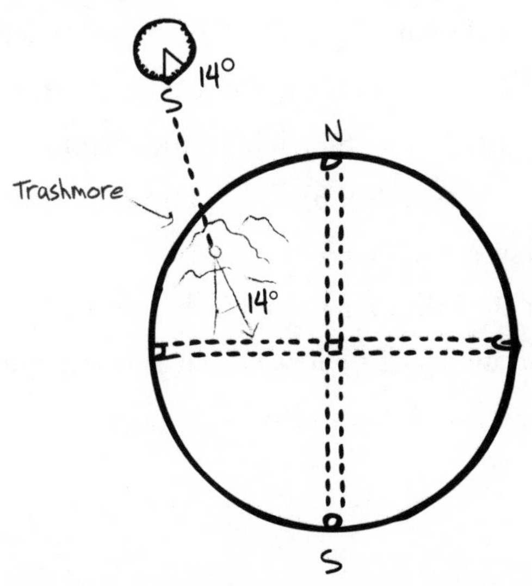

Using the compass, the map, and a flashlight, the three of them checked each of the tunnels that veered off from the room. Sure enough, only one of the openings had the 14-degree angle matching a slope of minus four, and they plunged in.

Ham had dug another small flashlight from his pocket and passed it to Di. The two of them had also scavenged hockey helmets from Trashmore; Tom Jones had wrapped a dirty sweatshirt around his capped head. The beams of light splashed up on the walls of the tunnel, showing rocky, jagged sides; the floor was fairly smooth. No way to tell if they were taking a straight line, so every twenty steps or so they checked the angle the tunnel was making with true south.

It was dead-on 14 degrees each time.

Di and Tom had calculated the number of paces that should bring them to the x-pipe. The Trashmore entrance was eight hundred yards above the x-axis. But the tunnel angled inward one hundred yards for every four hundred it moved downward, so by the time it hit the x-axis pipe it would have angled in two hundred yards. This formed a right triangle.

Using the triangle rule they had learned with the straws, they saw that $(2 \times 2) + (8 \times 8) =$ the third side, times itself. Multiplying, they got $4 + 64 = 68$.

This meant the third, long side was between 8 and 9. (To be exact, it was about 8.24 when Di put it in her calculator. Or, in yards, 824.) And that's what they found.

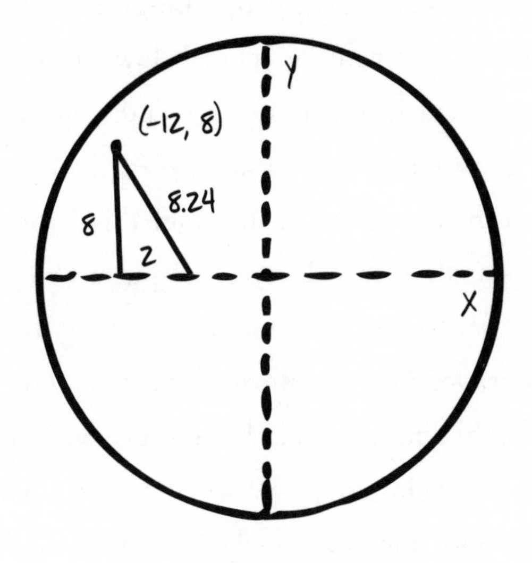

After 824 paces they arrived at a small, metal door, with a handle near the middle. The door was loose; it swung open easily—and they stepped down into a pool of bright light. Crouching in place, blinking for a few moments, they found themselves inside a massive pipe, tall enough to set up a basketball hoop and at least as wide.

The light was pouring in from their right, where the pipe broke through the cliffs like an open mouth. This was it, all right, the big east-west artery that they had found from above. The x-axis itself: They were now inside one of the pipes they had sat on under the outhouses.

It seemed as if no one had been through in ages. The pipe was cracked, dusty. Birds had nested out near the mouth and farther inside, leaving droppings everywhere. A mix of squawking and ruffling echoed down through the great tube. Tom, the first one in, jumped and windmilled his arms once—a gesture that Di had never seen.

"Oh yeah, we are *in*. We just done this!" Tom said.

Ham stared, with cold eyes. Di put a hand on his arm. Tom Jones wasn't losing his mind; he was happy.

Ham headed into the throat of the pipe, toward the plant, where the light dimmed to black, while Di and Tom checked the tunnels and openings opposite where they had entered. Some had small doors, and others looked like no more than cracks in the pipe. According to their map, the minus-four-slope tunnel should pick up on the other side of the x-axis, just opposite where it came in. Sure enough, the tunnel resumed with the same slope on the other side.

"Yeah, it's like I remember in there," Ham said, returning from the gloom. "They basically put up a thick, steel grate. It's totally cut off."

Tom flattened his map on the pipe wall. "Well," he said, "look at this. The entrance to the next tunnel is right where it's supposed to be, and shows where we should hit the intersection. Di, look. Ham."

The map showed clearly where they were and where they were going.

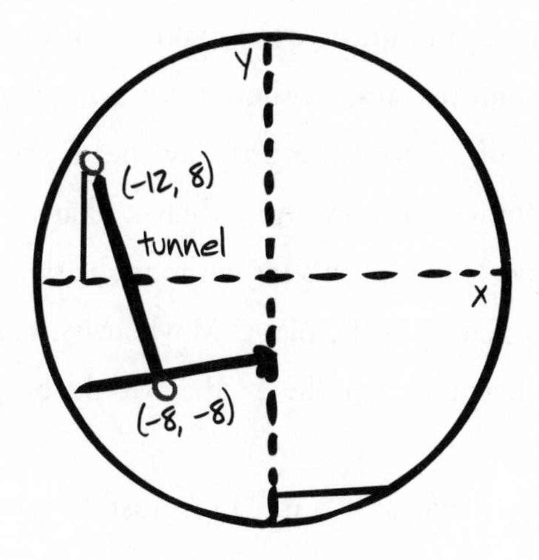

"Yeah, yeah," said Ham. "That looks right. With slopes, the higher the number, the steeper the line is. So if you have a fraction, it kind of goes flat, like this one does—" He stopped. "What are we doing?" he said to Tom. "Do you know where we're going? Do you know exactly? Because if you cannot track your butt back, Jones, you're dead. Worse. I'm not going another step until we mark everything, there and back. All the way back." The words poured out of Ham. He even had some color in his face, Di noticed, like a wax figure coming to life. Tom eyeballed him from under his cap, furious.

"Ham," said Di. Her voice seemed to relax the two of them, almost instantly. "Ham, listen. We have been following these clues for months or something, and it always seems like we can't figure them out, or we're making a mistake. Or you know, like it's not real and we should just give up or go back." She took a breath. But what exactly lay ahead? she wondered. The plant, almost certainly. And then—what? Mrs. Clarke would not have led them this far without a very good reason. What was happening at the plant? Maybe Mrs. Clarke would be waiting when they got there. That would be perfect, Di thought.

She looked back at Ham. "Let's just keep solving the problems in front of us, is that OK? That's all we have right now. And of course let's mark that door we came out of with the chalk."

That did it.

The tunnel Tom had chosen led straight back under Adjacent, according to the compass. Only it was rougher on this side of the pipe; there was no real floor, just a crumbly narrowing of the opening underneath. Slow moving at first, forearms on walls, and now there were animals scurrying, animals in the dark. Di could feel them and had no idea what they were.

Tom picked up the pace, and the two others kept up, Ham followed by Di. The seam was very narrow in places, then narrower, and soon became too tight to turn around. They were on their stomachs now, arms forward, wriggling like snakes. One more inch or two and they would be stuck,

Di thought; the whole island seemed to be pressing on her back.

"Tom!" The claustrophobia. She tried and tried to move her wrist, but there was no space and she could barely breathe. She realized she'd been trembling. She whispered to herself, "Just solve the problem, just solve the problem in front of you"—more Mrs. Clarke wisdom, which was feeling pretty weak down there. Turn off your brain, Di said to herself. Off. She dearly wished now that she had not talked Ham into following Tom. If they'd turned back they could have been at Polya's by now, sitting on the tires out back with cream sodas.

"It's blocked," she heard Tom say.

"What?" Ham said.

"The intersection point of the two tunnels," said Tom. "We're here. Minus eight, minus eight. But oh man, there's water here and it's caved in and I can't go any farther." He stopped and breathed heavily for a while and said: "Let's go back. We have to go back."

"Back? How?" said Ham, annoyed. "I can barely move forward."

Di was suddenly feeling dizzy.

"Damn!" Ham said. "I don't believe I'm down here again. I despise this place, every rock, every trailer, every Adjacent thing. OK, Jones, listen to me. That puddle you see, it's a U-shaped drop that sometimes fills up with water. You can drop down in there and come out the other side. Hold your breath, close your eyes—turn over first; you have to go in on your back, OK? And then you just kinda drop down in there and you can pull yourself up the other side. Make sure to put your arms forward, put them in first."

Di threw up a splash of BBQ flavor in her mouth. She swallowed hard, shuddered.

"No," Tom said. His voice was strange. Tom was not doing so well.

"What do you mean, no?"

"I mean, no. No, I can't do it. I won't do it."

"Uh-huh. You got a better idea? It's much wider and easier on the other side of this—once you're through there it's all easy and—"

"No."

"—look, I've got an idea. How about I come up there and ram your scrawny ass through myself. You know I would, and you know I would enjoy—"

Di heard a splashing sound. More splashing. Then quiet. She thought maybe Tom had yelled something but she didn't know. Her mind was blanking out. Eyes open? She checked and they were. Still conscious. Very important.

"OK, Lady Di, you heard what I said to him. Turn on your back, arms in first. Let yourself drop under the water and reach up with your hands on the other side and pull up. Don't worry about the flashlight; just make sure it's attached to your wrist. OK?"

"OK." She saw in the small, wavering light Ham's torso disappear down into the water; his waist and now feet were gone, and Di was alone. Alone now. Alone at the center of the earth.

She stared for a while at the rock just in front of her. Be a worm, she told herself. A worm. Worms live down here. Think of nothing else. She pushed off and pushed more, and then she was in. Cold, muddy, grainy water. Her back slid down into a smooth surface, almost like a deep bathtub, and for a half second she lay there. Just to feel the opening space. Her stinging lungs forced her to scrape to the surface on the other side—pray for it, she thought—and she was out. More space. Much more. Glory be: An actual tunnel! The $\frac{1}{5}$-slope tunnel was almost like a normal hallway in a house, she thought.

Tom and Ham, crouching, pulled her out and to her feet. Ham held her shoulders for a second, looked her straight in the eye, then made a fist and touched it to his forehead.

Was this some bizarre Ham solidarity gesture? Di instantly collapsed to the ground, snorting with laughter. In a second Tom was down there too, shivering and laughing so hard he could not breathe. She had not laughed this hard in her life, not even close.

It went on, and on. She stopped finally and felt a twinge of alarm about Ham. He wasn't on the ground laughing—where was he? She swept the flashlight around the small space and saw him, leaning against a wall, crossing himself. Several times. Then he turned, and Di saw from his face that he was OK.

They had made it through.

From there it was an easy walk through the ⅕ tunnel to the y-pipe. And there was no doubt about it, either: the same small, metal door, and on the other side a massive steel cylinder. Wider than the x-pipe, if anything, with many fewer cracks. Shiny, slick walls, with dozens of the little doors.

"This sucker's in use," said Ham.

The three of them walked along the pipe toward the outer edge of Folsom first, moving slowly to keep their footing.

At the end, this pipe, too, sloped downward and out to sea, like the x-pipe, only far more steeply: a forty-yard drop at least, it looked like. No one wanted to get close enough to check. One step too far and you would be shooting down to wherever.

According to their calculations, the pipe came out under the Point somewhere. It had an industrial odor, which soon caused a shifting sensation in Di's gut.

But before she could speak they all stopped and listened: What? A humming. Bigger than humming. A drumming noise. The drumming that had shaken Tom off the top of the pipe under the outhouse—*this pipe*—the loud thrum that had repeated in Ham's head ever since he'd first come into the tunnels, like some underground growl.

"Move, you suckers, back into the tunnel!" Ham screamed.

The rumble piled up on itself louder and crashed forward and the worst of it was that they were running back toward it with no footing and a horrible certainty that it was some dragon robot coming for their blood.

Ham pushed his soft body through the metal door and into the tunnel first, reaching one hand back. Di grabbed it, was pulled in, and left out a hand for Tom, who leaped up and into the tunnel going back: scratching forward, for dear life, back the way they came, the three of them.

It caught them, whatever it was. Shot up through the tunnel like a terrible tentacle that wrapped around their legs and then bubbled around them, hot and pungent and liquid, and then slipped back, seeping back toward the pipe. The pounding noise drove into their heads and chests and they were face down, screaming.

Tom reached up for his hat: It was there. Soaked. He made sure that he was still breathing, sniffed the hat—what was it? He could hear the others wheezing. He reached forward and felt Di's foot.

Ham was up ahead, moving, and said, "What the flying—"

"Water," Tom said. "It's hot water."

No one said anything more. The dragon-freight-train monster was, well, exactly what you would expect to be going through a pipe. Water, of all things. They all tried to walk along casually, shrugging a little, as if they knew it all along. Yet the thunder rolled and shook them as if from the inside. Of course it was water; some kind of cooling system for the plant; what else could it be? Di thought. It didn't matter to her much at that very moment; they had survived it, that's what was most important.

They moved quickly back along the ⅕ tunnel, dropped back through the U-shaped puddle—much easier this time but still a little hairy—and retraced every step. Back into and across the x-pipe and finally up the ladder under Trashmore. Tom was the last one up, and a thought stopped him. The water cannon: It had been quiet and suddenly started shooting. Why?

He thought for a moment about trying to get a closer look, before turning and ducking through the door. It was time to bail.

Still: Where did that water go?

VIRGIL

TOM JONES'S MOST CRUCIAL SKILL, IF YOU THOUGHT about it, was evasion. He was an escape artist. You'd see him cornered on the playground, or notice a couple of hoods waiting for him at his locker, and think: Uh-oh. Rene D. Quartez with his ripped muscles and Pascal Blasé with his spooky smile and even Ham for a while had all stalked him and swore they would light him up, or "pound your butt back to Arabia, Jones." Yet it never happened, not once.

On the bus to school one morning, a week or so after exploring the tunnels, Tom told Di how he did it. He studied people, he said, and most of all he studied places.

"Anyplace where I might get caught. The hallway. Empty classrooms. Corners of the schoolyard. That alleyway between the gym and the football fields. I find an escape route for almost every one. If I can't, I don't go there."

He knew how to bail through a window of the third-floor study hall (which was supposed to be for homework, but with no teachers present turned into a free-for-all). He knew where the holes in the schoolyard fence were, all of them. He knew how to lose someone quickly by zigzagging under the football stands. In Adjacent he knew which trailers he could slip under, which he could climb over. Most important of all, though, he said he knew how to disappear.

"What? Seriously? Even you're not that skinny," said Di.

All he had to do, he said, was take off his Angels hat and stand up straight. "And then no one knows who I am. Or at least, it takes them a while to recognize me. They don't even really see me, and I'm gone before they realize it," he said. "Look."

Off came the cap.

"Ohh!" Di said. She almost shrieked. "You have a forehead! And hair! I can't believe it, you look like that kid on that TV show"—she was starting to giggle. His eyes were bigger than she had realized, his face stronger somehow. He looked from the side like his dad—masculine, even handsome—though she would never tell him that.

"Clam it, would you?" he said. He had the hat back in place. He wasn't smiling. As the bus pulled into the schoolyard some of the younger kids shifted in their seats and stared out the corner of their eyes. Something was up. Tom saw it immediately: The Poets had set up a perimeter, with at least six of them posted in a loose circle, waiting for the bus.

"Are they coming for us?" Di said.

"I'm not going to wait to find out."

As the doors opened Tom told Di to follow him. He slipped off his hat, put his chin in the air, and once off the bus slipped into a loose, moving clutch of older kids that included Pascal. He reached back a hand to pull Di with him, but she resisted.

"No, no—you go, we're splitting up—they won't pick on a girl out here," she said. She watched him turn and bury himself in the group, moving like a shadow, in the group but not one of them. He separated, sliced through the churning mobs of arriving students, and angled over to a pickup basketball game at the edge of the yard.

It all happened in a matter of seconds. The Poets, who knew the two were friends, apparently wanted them both. When they realized she was alone, they turned to sweep the schoolyard for signs of a red cap, a thin dark figure in baggy clothes. Too late. After jumping for a rebound in traffic under the hoop, Tom had crashed himself into the chain-link fence behind the basket, and pushed himself through a narrow opening at the corner of the fence. He dropped from there down the sloping hill behind the yellow-brick school building, and moved into the building's shadow.

He had disappeared again, gone.

Up in the yard, the Poets had split, with three fanning out through the yard to look for Tom and three others closing on Di. She was too heavy and awkward to imitate Tom's slipperiness, and there was no hiding her orange hair. She made for the main school entrance, where at least there should be a security guard. Should be, but wasn't; there were only students, massing at the door, pushing to get inside.

Di knew she was trapped. She swung around, her back to the brick, just outside the gray arch over the school doors.

It was Virgil, and two others behind him. She recognized them: his hard-looking girlfriend, Joy C. James, a kid in some of her classes they called Vegan, and another face she'd seen in the school hallway. She looked wildly around and saw that most everyone was inside. It was past the bell.

Virgil squinted and said, "Hey, pork buns, time for a vocabulary lesson." He whispered in her ear. Ugly words. She wasn't sure what they even meant, but his voice was disgusting, cruel as an eye gouge. "Do you talk about those things with your little Arabian knight friend, huh?"

She was paralyzed. She had never been cornered like this by boys, and wondered: Is this what it's like being Tom? Being a smaller boy?

"So you think I'm funny, and you're going to spit in my eye?!" Virgil hissed. "And I don't even know you, you fatty little island slug."

She tried to shake her head to say she was sorry but it didn't move.

Virgil narrowed one eye and spat on her shoes. It dripped. It felt like the most disgusting thing ever in the history of her entire life, maybe of mankind. Thick soaking snot from the mouth of a poisonous snake. She still could not speak or move and for a floating moment it all seemed unreal, like she was seeing it in a movie.

Virgil glanced at the other two, whose faces Di did not care to look at. They would look so puffy and ugly and satisfied.

Now stepping closer to her, his glass eye as cold and slimy as a gecko's, Virgil stared. It was endless, it was worse than being trapped in a cave, it seemed like forever was passing: Wasn't school out yet?

"Poetry," he was saying, hissing again. "You ever, ever humiliate me again—if you ever *look* at me—I'm going to punish you with poetry."

She had no idea what he was talking about. She would have told him anything he wanted if she could've made a sound. And now Virgil was talking again and she couldn't really hear him and her eyes felt warm. She hated herself for it, hated how the tears were dripping down her face into her mouth. She wanted so badly for everything to be over: this, the tunnels, all of it.

"*Mr. Wilfred!*" Mr. Washington's voice. A huge hall security monitor. A miracle. His voice boomed again. "What were you going to do, son, beat up a seventh grader? With three friends? Very brave, Mr. Wilfred. Come with me, you four." He turned to Di. "Young lady, are you going to be OK?"

Di nodded weakly.

He waited a beat or two. "All right, you may proceed to class. I'll send a note to your teacher." Di twirled her wrist slowly, and felt herself reinhabiting her body, when she saw on the ground a Swiss Army knife. Without thinking she picked it up, slipped it into her pocket—and froze.

Mr. Washington was looking back at her, herding the Poets in front of him with huge arms. Had he seen? Why on earth had she picked up the stupid knife? Having any weapon at school was grounds for suspension. Now she had one in her front pocket: It had to belong to one of the Poets. She hadn't seen her own Swiss Army knife in months.

"You're sure you're OK to find your class?" the security guard said.

"Uh, good—yes!" Di said.

She was exhausted. So completely spent that she wanted to find an empty classroom and sleep on the floor. Instead she had to join Mrs. Johnson's class, history.

First period: not even one class period had passed in the time she was held hostage! She slipped into the class without anyone taking much notice. It had a back door, near her desk, and Mrs. Johnson had no control. The class was a free-for-all of gossip, note passing, rubber band shooting, and—by far the worst hazard—spitballs. Some kids made tiny ones, which they shot through pen casings, usually at other students' foreheads.

Other kids made giant spitballs, by stuffing entire sheets of paper in their mouths at the beginning of class. By the end they had dense, compact splatter bombs that—when Mrs. Johnson turned her back—they would lob at a wall or window, and even sometimes the blackboard if a student was up there trying to explain something. These things hit like a wet snowball and usually brought the class to a full stop, while Mrs. Johnson stalked around and asked who did it. No one was ever really sure, because the good spitballers were almost impossible to catch in the act.

Di heard one of the BB-size spitballs fly past her ear. She almost wanted to be hit, she was so anxious and bored. She looked through the windows for any sign of Tom. Nothing. She wondered where he'd gone. He'd have to get back in somehow and find his way back on the bus. His dad would accept no excuse for missing class, absolutely none.

She glanced back up at the clock. One minute had passed

since she last looked—one. Could the clock be stuck? No. The minute hand jerked forward suddenly.

"Miss Smith. Perhaps you could tell us a little about Sam Houston?"

Her heart lept. Houston? Sam Houston? A few loose facts bubbled up into her head, from the previous night's reading. Houston was a city, she knew, named after Mr. Houston. Or was it the other way around? Or was that just buck-naked wrong? She had to go with it.

"Um, Sam Houston, who they named the city of Houston after? Houston, Texas? He was a president of the state who helped get independence, and winning some land from Mexico, or Spain, and he was very important."

She waited for the laughter. Nothing. She braced for a spitball, maybe a snowball. It didn't come.

"That's right, that's a start," Mrs. Johnson said. "Mr. Davis, maybe you could pick up from there. Tell us more."

Di nearly fainted with relief. She opened her notebook to appear more scholarly but the next thing she knew she'd begun to doodle, without really thinking, just shapes and lines. She sketched, and half-slept in her chair, for what felt like a long time, and checked the clock again: The minute hand had clunked forward another notch. She groaned and slid down in her chair. As she let her eyes close for a short nap, a BB spitball pinged in her ear, and lodged there. She opened her eyes and tried to get the damp thing out. No luck.

She gave up and stared back down at her notebook. She was surprised to see that she had drawn a map of the island. Adjacent here, the plant over there, the x- and y-pipes, and the tunnels they had found. She stared at it and wrote down the symbols:

$m = -4$

$m = 1/5$

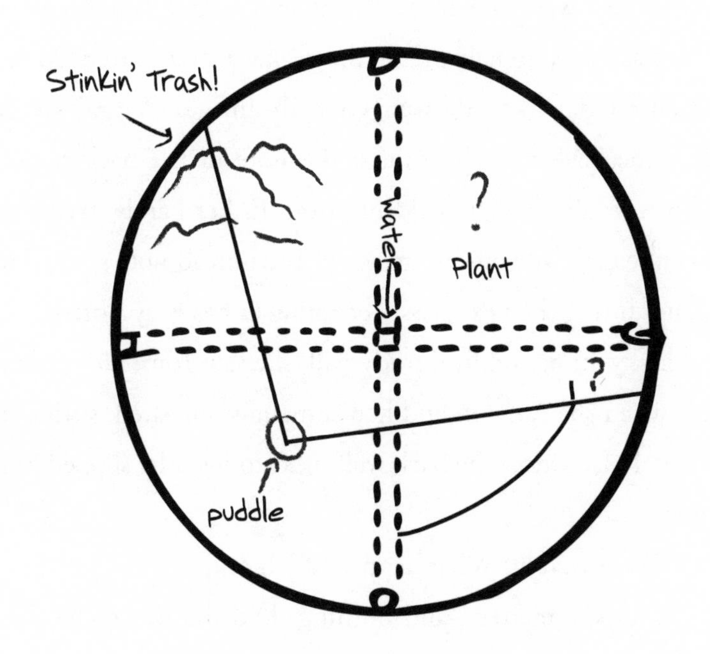

And then something in her head slid into place. She had seen this shape before. Many times, drawn by someone other than Tom. Where? Who? She couldn't remember. She ransacked her memory and couldn't place it.

The day slowed to a near stop again in periods two and three, and she remembered the knife. She had to get rid of it. In the hallway chaos between classes she casually dropped it into a trashcan and felt instantly better.

She stopped by her locker after lunch—still no sight of Tom—and was rummaging around in a side pocket of her backpack when she noticed a small, red envelope.

Maybe it was from Tom, she thought, and pulled it out.

It was folded in half and on the back were two letters, M.K., written in red marker. She went cold. The image of Virgil's savage face came back and she stuffed the note in her back pocket without reading it. She held her head in her hands, trying to shake the chill. It wouldn't go away. The unread note seemed to expand during the next class, becoming as heavy as a brick.

Finally, in period five, study hall, she saw Tom. He was not there when she came in and had somehow appeared, sitting in his usual place, near the back wall, next to her. She slipped him a note.

"Where were u? What happened?" it said.

"It doesn't matter—and nothing. Did the EPs come after you?"

"Yes!!!" she wrote back. "And someone left me a note. I've been too freaked to read it." She passed him the note. He read it, tightened, and passed it back. Di finally forced herself to look. But it wasn't from the Poets. It read:

(11) 6 × 7

"Someone just passed us another clue," she whispered.

"Huh, a smiley face?" said Tom.

"Maybe it's an eleven, you know, underlined?" Di sighed. "What's going on? Who could have given us this?"

THE POINT

YOU SOMETIMES HEARD SOME LAME CROUTON—THAT'S what we called Crotona people—trying to be polite about Adjacent. You'd be at the mall, or a school football game, and hear something like, "Oh, I don't know, Miriam, this is terrible to say, but I just think those kids are a little slow, that's all. Maybe it's the poverty. Or the toxins."

You were dying to say: Miriam! OK, true, we are a pack of desperate dirtballs who have pulled some of the most idiotic stunts on earth out of sheer boredom. You would be too, if you lived your entire life trapped between a towering mountain of garbage and a foul nuclear plant.

But slow? Rene D. Quartez built an all-terrain vehicle out of parts he stripped from old cars. Pascal knew everything about medical stuff. Theonta Hutchison had probably been the best student at TriCounty Middle and High School. And we had this kid called Oki Koulu who was better at computers than anyone from that gomer ranch, the Crotona Gifted Scholars Program.

Besides, there's another kind of slow, the kind where you're kicking around, doing nothing at all, but your brain's got a couple things in the slow cooker. You need some good slow time to work out real problems, and Di and Tom finally got some that next weekend.

They were back at the Point, sitting in the rock couch and staring out to sea in silence. The only thing moving on the horizon was a small black figure with a surfboard, thrashing in the heavy swell: Blue Moon, king of all dangerous lunatics, out for his morning fight against death. Di had never seen him actually surf on a wave before. At the moment, she was actually channeling some vintage Mrs. Clarke advice—*If the problem is too big, solve a smaller piece of it. If that's too hard, solve something that looks similar. Solve what's in front of you; solve what you can. Look at what's in front of you*—when Tom broke the silence.

"Have we used all the information? That's what Mrs. Clarke would say about now, you know."

Di nodded. "Well, let's think about it. There's no way she could have crawled around and left those clues underground at the last second. She must have planted them in advance, knowing something could happen."

Tom squinted out at Blue Moon, and over the horizon. Sea

and sky faced each other like two shimmering mirrors, and Tom's mind was sweeping easily through the many possibilities. "But why wouldn't she go to the police?" he said. "Not that they would listen to anyone from Adjacent, but they did come out here after Rene's mom first disappeared. She must not have trusted anyone but us. Well, us and whoever passed us that last clue."

Di sighed. Who on earth would Mrs. Clarke trust with something like this? Not a kid; a kid would have blabbed by now.

The wind shifted, and a mist from the breakers below cooled their faces. "She wants us to do something, Tom," Di said. "At the plant. It has to be. Mr. Pink, the security guy, they're all plant people. Maybe she wants us to stop them from doing something. My theory"—and here she looked very serious—"my theory is that maybe they're planning to blow up the island."

Tom looked her square in the eyes before tipping over and shaking with laughter. "Excuse me, Di, but aren't they *on* the island?"

She felt a twinge of annoyance before smiling herself—no, the plant wasn't going to blow itself up—and the pair sat there for a long while doing nothing at all, suspended in that rock seam between sea and sky.

"Wait. Look!" Tom shouted. He was pointing down toward the water, almost laughing. "Look. Down there. It's the pipe! That's the y-pipe, where the water comes out. The pipe is right under the ground until it gets near the edge—remember?—where it angles down. It had to come out somewhere. Look, you can see water coming out now."

Sure enough, there it was, looking from this distance as harmless as anything. There all along, hidden in plain sight.

"That water doesn't come out all the time. We know it turns on and off. And I think maybe there's someone in Adjacent who has an idea when," Tom said. Di glanced out toward the sea, suddenly alarmed. Her wrist began to twirl.

"Hey, no. I'm not going to talk to Blue Moon, I don't care what happens."

"Not him," Tom said. "I'm thinking of someone else. Someone you could talk to. Someone who knows all about the waves."

Unlike Ham Rowan, who had become quiet, soft, and passive after his adventure, Thea Hutchison—the girl who had almost died after water-skiing behind the ferry—had become quiet and angry after hers. She spent hours roaming the rocks and small coves at the base of the island, like she was falling in love with the place where she almost died. She was the only person other than Blue Moon who would go down there. When she wasn't down scaling the rocks of the island, she was up in her backyard, working out—boxing, usually, as she was doing that morning, when Di found her behind her trailer.

"Hey," Di said.

The older girl grunted. A junior, taller than many adults,

she was hitting a heavy burlap bag, which was hanging from a hook on a telephone pole. The sun was low in the sky, and in the blinding glare, Thea looked like some mythical shadow warrior. Di shielded her eyes and spoke loudly. "Thea—hello!"

Thea turned and nodded, annoyed.

Di raised her voice again. "Thea, listen, I'm going to tell you something, OK? You can keep boxing, just listen. Me and Tom—Tom Jones, you know?—we need to get into the plant. Into Folsom. Something bad is happening there, or is going to happen, and we know how to get inside the place, I think. But we need your help. We need to figure out when it's safe to crawl through that big water pipe. We risked our lives in there."

Thea did not answer or even turn to look at Di. She stopped hitting the bag for a moment and took a breath. In the month or so since her near drowning many people had offered to help her, had advised her, lectured her; one even gave her the name of a psychiatrist in Crotona. Until now, no one had asked her for her help.

"Look, I helped you with the surfboard, remember—"

"Water ski."

"Water ski. Whatever. I borrowed tools for you from my mom's toolbox—"

"Not right now," Thea said. "I'm not saying never. I'm saying not now. You got some nerve coming right up to me, after what I been through. You're crazier than you look. But I'm in no kind of helping mood right now, I don't care what you're problems are.

Leave me be. I'm not always like this, I'm just—well, I am a lot of the time."

With that she turned back to the punching bag.

Di returned later that day, and regularly after many school days. Sometimes Thea was around and willing to talk; most of the time she wasn't. Di wanted to let it go but eventually decided that she'd spent too much time on Thea to give up. Besides, she didn't know what else to do: They needed to know more about the y-pipe before trying to crawl through it again. And one day, out of the deep blue, Thea turned to the pudgy redhead in her backyard and said, "OK. I'll take you down. We're going down. You been good to stay with me like this, and I feel like—I don't know. Just give me a few minutes to get ready, and I'll meet you by the Point."

Di raced to find Tom, and soon the two friends were following big Thea Hutchison around the outside of the chain-link fence at the Point and back where the two cliffs that banked the cove came together in a large V shape. It looked like a sheer drop down to the rocks, but the cliffs were close enough that you could use them to support yourself going down, and it wasn't nearly as steep as it looked.

Thea showed them how. In minutes they were standing on one of the large rocks at the base of the cove, watching foaming layers of white water swirl at their feet. The pool below the pipe was far deeper and wider than it appeared from above; a tugboat could easily pull in here, Tom thought. The mouth of the y-pipe was clearly visible now, jutting out of the cliff to their left, spitting water into the cove. Di and Tom immediately noticed something about it: The opening was very low. The water level in the cove was just under the lower lip of the pipe.

"Tide's coming in," Thea said. "Another hour or so and the water will almost cover this rock we're standing on here."

"Really? It will come up above that pipe?" Di said.

"Of course. Didn't I just tell you that it covers this here rock? It fills up the last few feet of the pipe—the part that angles down—at high tide, for about an hour or so. Depending on how high the high tide is, of course."

"Why?" Di looked over at Tom, then at Thea. "What do you mean how high the tide is?"

"I mean that sometimes the high tide is eight feet or so, and comes up to there"—she pointed to a line just under the pipe—"and sometimes it's closer to fourteen feet and up to here"—she held her hand palm down, near her knees and well above the pipe mouth.

"So the pipe doesn't flush out water when it's up that high?" Di said.

"Obviously, Einstein. It would back up badly. It's like trying to pour water through a straw that's sitting in a glass of soda. Some of the water might go through but it starts to come back up the straw. This is the Folsom cooling system. It sucks in water at the other side near the ferries—I know that because I saw it up close and almost got sucked in there—and it shuts down automatically when it senses the mouth of the pipe is blocked," she said.

She paused there and added, in a softer voice, "And it passes through and comes out this side hot."

"That," said Tom, "we know."

Thea swung around and faced Tom and looked at him for the first time. "Come again, little man?"

Di told her everything. She and Tom had not agreed beforehand to do this but they needed help and it seemed like the right thing to do. Their plans were safe enough with Thea. People were no more likely to believe her than Ham. Both had been written off as mental cases, even though Thea had been a very good student and a reliable person before her accident.

In turn, Thea told them all about the tide. How it filled in twice a day, about twelve hours apart. How high tide was about an hour later each day—today it came at one o'clock, tomorrow it would be at two o'clock. And how every sixteen days or so the tide came in very high, well over the mouth of the pipe.

"If you want to go in the pipe and have some time, you need to figure out what day, at what time, the high high tide comes in," Thea said. "Just make a chart, it's easy."

"How? I mean, could you show us?" Di said.

Thea reached into her backpack and pulled out a small notebook. She was annoyed, Di noticed, as if she couldn't believe she was sharing this information. She opened it and showed them several pages of dense, scrawled calculations.

"See? Just come down here and keep track. Any stupid clown could do it, OK? Now, I'm going back."

"NO!" said Di. Her ears had turned scarlet, and she moved to block Thea from the path back up. "Don't say we're stupid! We've figured out everything so far!" She took a breath. "Look," she said, not yelling now. "We just don't know how to do this. We haven't seen it before, that's all."

Thea had put her notebook away and was now trying to suppress a smile, Di noticed, like she was babysitting two kindergartners or something.

"You know what?" Di said. "That ferry that cut you loose? That was a Folsom ferry. Folsom. The plant, maybe you've heard of it? They're the people who are making people disappear and searching everyone's homes. They searched yours too, I bet. Went through your parents' bedroom, and your brother's."

Thea was no longer smiling. She stood for a long time, silent, staring back up at the cliffs. It was here in this cove, after being swept halfway around the island by the currents, after being buried repeatedly under mountains of water—here where she had finally found her way back to shore after the water-skiing attempt. Dumb luck is all it was. Her will had run out about fifty yards off shore when an easy-roller of a wave picked her up and bodysurfed her in.

"OK," she said. "Today, high tide was at eight o'clock in the morning. Well, eight in the morning and eight at night: two high tides, understand? A.M. and P.M. That means tomorrow it will be at nine o'clock. OK?"

She explained further. "Write down today's date and the time of high tide: November first, eight o'clock. Then chart the whole month: November second, third, fourth, and so on, and beside each date the time of the tide. Finally, track the highest high tide, which comes about every sixteen days, on the same chart.

"Today's is very high. I know that because I've been keeping track," Thea continued. "So the high high tide will be back in sixteen days. Here's what that would look like. This is not exact to the minute, but it's close enough."

Date	Time of high tides	Level of high tides
Nov. 1	8am, 8pm	highest
Nov. 2	9am, 9pm	
Nov. 3	10am, 10pm	
Nov. 4	11am, 11pm	
Nov. 5	12am, 12pm	
Nov. 6	1am, 1pm	
Nov. 7	2am, 2pm	
Nov. 8	3am, 3pm	lowest
Nov. 9	4am, 4pm	
Nov. 10	5am, 5pm	
Nov. 11	6am, 6pm	
Nov. 12	7am, 7pm	
Nov. 13	8am, 8pm	
Nov. 14	9am, 9pm	
Nov. 15	10am, 10pm	
Nov. 16	11am, 11pm	highest

Tom studied the chart. He saw that they would have to match the high high tide with a time when he and Di and Ham were free, either on the weekend or in the afternoon after school.

"So the highest high tide is the best time, I see that," he said. "But the level of high tide kind of rises, right, and then drops again?"

"Right," Thea said.

"So the day of the highest tide—is that the only day the pipe mouth is blocked?"

"Good. No, it's not. You got about three days on either side of that highest tide where the pipe is covered, for at least a half hour, maybe more."

Di and Tom knelt over the chart. Two fingers pointed at the same day: the week after Wednesday.

VISITORS FROM TOWN

WHEN SOMETHING UGLY IS ABOUT TO GO DOWN, SOME heinous rumble or fight, it seems like every kid in school can feel it coming. The jocks and the French club and the chess team and of course the hoodlums all know it; even the beautiful people, who are always hugging themselves and each other and wearing Italian sneakers or whatever, know it. Seriously, you could grab the most severe pinhead from the seventh-grade class and lock him in a basement room with nothing but a documentary about the Antarctic or the Kalahari Desert and he would know something's coming.

The most ominous sign at TriCounty was that the Poets had backed off completely. Suddenly they had no interest at all in the islanders.

Di sensed the danger, like everyone else, and was busy

imagining all the plots the Poets might be planning when Mr. Sternberg, the tech research teacher, hit her with a question:

"Miss Smith, have you fully arrived yet? Maybe you could tell the class how to begin researching something online. Where would you start?"

It was fourth period, when we usually had a break in the afternoon. The work was easy, simple online tricks for finding information that most of the kids already knew. The annoying part was that the computers were as old and slow as those in Adjacent and took forever to connect to the Internet. If they connected at all. Mr. Sternberg usually illustrated the searches on handouts, which no one ever read.

"I would go to a search engine, uh, and start searching for . . . probably an encyclopedia maybe, like an information site?"

"Right," Mr. Sternberg said, smiling. "That's a good start. Begin by searching these reference sources"—he handed out another printout, which was stuffed into backpacks never to be retrieved—"and then if there are things in those entries you don't understand, you can look those up."

He looked around the class and stared down a spitballer in the back. "Now, I want you to take some time and research anything you like—sports, music, history, whatever it is—and just pull out some of the odd, unexpected, or interesting facts on the subject. Not the boring stuff. I'll hand out books for those of you whose computers aren't working."

The assignment was a gift for Di. Her computer, after freezing repeatedly, actually connected to the Internet. She found a reference site and, without really expecting any answer, typed in a single word: "circle." The island map she'd drawn that day in class was circular, and she still had a vague sense that she'd seen the map before.

And just like that, the key to the (11) 6 × 7 clue she'd found in her backpack tumbled loose.

She read a few things that were familiar, at first. The distance around a circle was called the circumference. The distance from one edge to the other through the center was called the diameter. The distance from the center point to the edge was the radius.

There was a simple diagram of this:

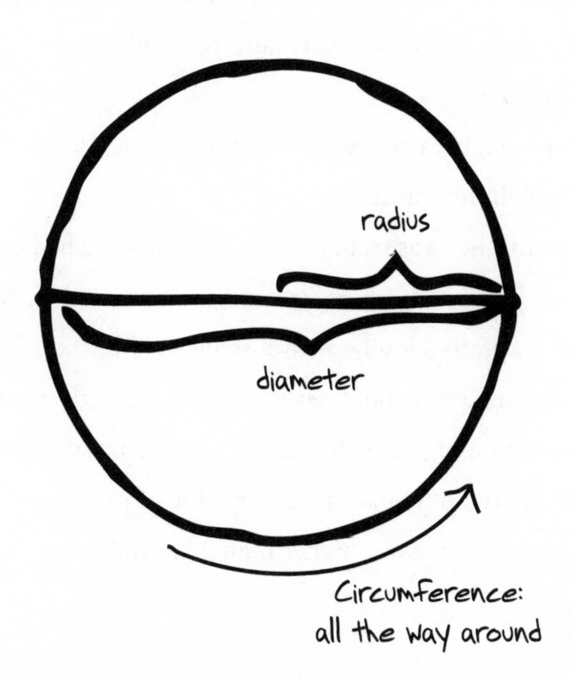

The site said that the circumference of any circle divided by the diameter was always the same number. She had heard of that number too. It was called pi. In Mr. Williams's class she had learned that the area of a circle—the amount of space inside it—was pi times the radius, times the radius again. That was true for any circle, of any size. The equation was simple: πr^2. Pi r squared. The site said a rough estimate of pi was 3.141593. Rough estimate?

Di sighed. This was all textbook information, boring math facts. Except that there was something strange going on with the circle, very strange, and it was bugging her. She couldn't pin it down. She reread the first few paragraphs and read on farther.

A circle was a circle—nothing weird there. Trace around the edge of a coin, a DVD, a plate, and you had one.

It wasn't that.

She peeled her eyes away from the screen. Closed them. Let all go black in her head. Pi.

That number was stranger than anything she had ever heard about in math, or anywhere else. It was a real number. You could measure it, pretty closely, with a string and a ruler. But if you had a true circle you could never measure it exactly, the site said. Ever. The value of 3.141593 was a "rough estimate" because no one had figured out what the exact value of pi was.

The actual value was higher than $3\,^1\!/_{10}$ and lower than $3\,^2\!/_{10}$.

In fact you could keep creeping closer to it like that and never get to it. How was that possible? It was there but not there.

She read on:

> Pi is what mathematicians call a transcendental number. That is, it cannot be expressed by a finite series of numbers or equations: It exists but cannot be found. The ratio begins with the numbers 3.141593 and goes on infinitely, with no recognizable pattern. Scholars have been trying for centuries to calculate it precisely, some believing that pi contains a hidden code, or could reveal an unseen order in the universe. Even a message from God.

She looked up.

She double-checked the Web site to make sure it wasn't some cult site. It wasn't. It was a university site. Those were sometimes reliable. She looked around quickly, ready to be embarrassed, or zinged with a spitball. No one was watching her.

She read more:

> The first known reference to it is in a Middle Kingdom scroll that dates to 1650

BC. A mathematician named Ahmes, writing about "The Entrance into the Knowledge of All Living Things," calculated the area of a circle, using a rough estimate of pi. Since then some of the best number theorists in the world have attempted to calculate pi or find some patterns in its numbers. None has succeeded.

The first person to use the Greek letter π for pi, the site said, was an English mathematician named William Jones.

Jones.

That did it. The sight of "pi" and "Jones" in the same sentence made Di catch her breath. The underlined eleven was not an eleven at all. It was the pi symbol. They had been reading the clue upside down. She took the paper out of her pocket and turned it around. It now read:

$2 \times 9 \; (\pi)$

A circle. Pi had to mean a circle. The tunnel or tunnels on the other side of the y-pipe would be circular. She looked up. She had lost all track of time. Mr. Sternberg was collecting papers, and the period was ending. She scrawled out some of what she had read about pi, now imprinted on her memory, and handed that in.

"Pi," she said to Tom when she took her seat, finally, on the bus home.

She said it again: "Pi. Pi, pi, pi. Pi."

It took a moment for the word to sink in with Tom, but his eyes narrowed beneath the cap, Di thought.

"Pi. You know. We heard about it in class? The underlined eleven on the note. It's the pi symbol. Not eleven. We were looking at it upside down. Think about it. A circle."

He looked up at her and slapped his hand on the top of his head.

"Oh, man," he said. "What idiots. What clowns. That has to be it."

He pulled his cap down low, and the two of them stared ahead. Pi, two, nine. Divided by? Multiplied by? And did that X mean another intersection?

The possible combinations lined up in their heads and reshuffled themselves, so absorbing their minds that they didn't notice crossing the bridge, or how low the sun was over the water. The days were getting shorter, fall shading by degrees into winter, and both had homework to do before it got dark that night.

That night—she would never forget it, as long as she lived.

Di had rice, beans, and tuna on tortillas for dinner and could tell that her mom was very upset. Silent, looking exhausted, Mrs. Smith told Di to skip the dishes, and grab some money for ice cream sandwiches from the jar.

"I'm going to lie down myself," she said. "I've had a bad day. A bad week. Make sure you pull the door closed when you come in."

Di found Tom outside Polya's, and they ate their deserts in silence. If she ever did escape Adjacent, she thought, she would miss this, just hanging outside Polya's as the sky turned purple and black. The stars out, the sea breathing on your neck, and Adjacent with its scattering of warm lights like the last stop before the abyss, an outpost on the shoulder of the earth, a misfit colony at the end of time. Her colony.

When the ice cream spell broke, Di suggested that they head over toward Ham's to see what he was thinking.

They never got there.

In the dying twilight, as they strolled along the plant road, they heard a car coming. The two of them instinctively stopped and turned, curious, and saw the headlights bob and swerve: This car was flying toward Adjacent, whoever it was. Di saw the danger first. The wasted glow of the gas-station light just outside the park illuminated a large convertible, full of high school kids. And she saw the unmistakable silhouette of Virgil, half-standing in the front passenger seat.

"Go go go go—tear!" she screamed at Tom. The car skidded to a stop in a hail of gravel, and Virgil, Vegan, and several others poured over the side and came at a dead run. Di and Tom split and scurried with all their might toward the nearest trailer. Di could smell the breath of one of the gang as she hit the ground and rolled under a trailer. The older boy dropped to his knees and plowed through the crawl space, knocking over boxes and pails and junk.

Di scratched out to the other side, but the bigger boy's hand flew out from under the trailer, locked around her ankle for a terrible second, before the grip broke and, stumbling, Di threw herself between two more trailers. She leaped up onto a garbage can, pushed off the top of a fence and onto the roof of a trailer, and dropped to all fours. She could hear two people down below, closing on her. She would not last long; she was agile but heavy and slow compared to the Poets.

"We have no issue with you, little Princess or whatever your name is; we want the knife, the Swiss Army knife," yelled one of them. She heard the other boy moving, looking for a way up. She wished she had not thrown it out! Why did she ever pick it up in the first place?

"We know you have it. We want it back, and don't even think of blackmailing Virgil. Otherwise we'll take you and your friend back with us and you don't want to know what will happen to you," the older boy said.

Di heard a clang behind her and knew one of them was on the garbage cans. She looked around wildly. It was dark but she could see another form moving on the roofs: Tom. He was up topside too, and scampering, with a bigger kid stumbling two trailers back behind him. She stayed low and scrambled toward a neighboring roof and pitched herself across. She felt at least one body up moving behind her, and could see another bigger form off to her right, and faked to one side, then cut back, and onto another roof—the Penfields', slick and aluminum—skittered across that and cut to her left again, bounced off the Rowans' roof, leaped out and caught a pole and swung to another roof.

A crash turned her around—her pursuer was down—and the boy swung back around to look for Di and saw her duck off of the Jacobis' roof and out of sight. The boy, it looked like one of the older Poets, was cursing, on his knees on another aluminum top, unsure which way to turn.

She felt a surge of energy, spun around, and kept moving, from one roof to another, zigging here, zagging back, following Tom out of the corner of her eye. The Poets were still following them on the ground, cutting through yards; the hounds were going crazy; and Di and Tom both angled toward the Quartez unit, where some of the older kids might be out. There were only so many roofs, and the Poets were athletic and angry—Di and Tom needed some help, and they knew it.

The two of them made it to the edge of the Quartez clearing area and stopped cold, dropping to their stomachs.

The courtyard-like opening in front of the Quartezes' was now flooded with moonlight. Di could see the convertible off in the background, near the road, its doors still hanging open. She could see people's faces looking out of trailer windows, afraid. And now there was nowhere else to go. She and Tom were trapped on these roofs.

Directly below them, out in the open now, were Virgil; his girlfriend, Joy; a kid they called Milton; and a few others, closing on them in a tightening circle.

This was it, Di knew. She tried to close her eyes. No luck, they were pinned open. She covered them with her hands and waited, one second, and two, and then there was a sound—a soft thud, and another. She peeked between her fingers. Rene D. Quartez had dropped from a roof somewhere and into the clearing. She heard a whirring sound and Pascal Blasé spun from the darkness into the clearing, in a motorized wheelchair; he was always faking injuries, and must have gotten the chair from his mom, a nurse. And here were other dark forms that moved out from shadows into the pale light—who? Thea was one. And Ham.

"Oh look, it's the Epic Clowns, come to the wrong neighborhood." Rene D.'s voice, and Di could see everything right below her perch, moving in sickly light as if in a fever: The faces of Virgil and the others. The falcon tattoo on Rene D.'s neck. The twitching in Ham's cheeks. Every speck of dirt in the air, suspended in silver light. Stardust, Adjacent's own ashes.

She saw that one of the Poets had a crowbar: a fat kid, someone she didn't know, and now they were moving forward to do—what? She went blank, no thoughts, nothing; she only knew she was breathing.

"The misfit freakin' toys," Virgil snorted. "Those two little punks got something of ours and we're going to take it back."

"Uh-huh," Rene D. said. "How 'bout you take these limp clowns home and put them to bed or you all go back in pieces."

Pascal revved the wheelchair motor. He was smiling insanely.

"Rene D." Sarcastic now. "Why don't you just hand them over and make it easy on yourself. If not we'll get them at school. And you know we will."

"I find out you put one hand on Lady Di or Tom Jones and I will hunt you down in your house," Rene D. said.

Di and Tom exchanged a look of awe. They didn't think that Rene D. knew they existed, much less their names.

"Now," he continued, "you got five seconds to turn around and get out." And he began counting.

The Poets only moved closer by about a half-step. The heavy kid with the crowbar looked scared and he was going to swing it, Di could feel that. Thea looked like a statue: She was focused like a laser on the crowbar. Ham was fingering something in his pocket and looked almost happy; he was regaining his insanity.

At the number four the scene froze. Something happened to the light, a slight change, like a porch light flicking off—where?—somewhere behind, back by Mr. Devlin's, off near Mrs. Clarke's.

Di felt a large shadow move behind her, wheeled around and saw nothing, then heard a muffled scream—and looked up to see the Poets turn and run wildly toward their car. Rene D., Pascal, and the others had scattered.

"What?" she said—and pushed up to her knees.

The convertible spun its wheels in the gravel, bumped back onto the road, and picked up speed. The Poets were scrambling, barely in the car, still pulling the passenger door closed when Di saw what they saw. A huge man shot out into the dusty light behind the car—sprinting in bare feet, long white Medusa snakes of hair flying behind him, moving faster than the car.

Blue Moon.

The old man caught the car from behind, slammed a huge paw over the lip of the convertible well and pulled himself up on the trunk and almost in. For a breath, Di was afraid for the passengers. But the car swung a hard turn—and threw its extra cargo into the darkness.

Di and Tom were now standing on the roof of a trailer, staring at the road. All of Adjacent, it seemed, was doing the same, waiting to see what the old lunatic would do next.

He did not disappoint them. He stumbled back out into the road like a wounded bear, threw his head back, and unleashed a noise so loud and deep and strange that some hounds began to howl and others cowered under trailers. Now another: louder still, angrier, and when he stopped, every hound on the island was hiding under something. A sea monster, a squid from the deep is what he was, far more terrible in person than people ever knew. And he sat down in the road after all that, folded his legs in some kind of yoga position, and started to meditate. Or maybe pray. Like some sick savage something, spilled out in the road.

Di looked down at her wrist to see if she could move it. She could. Meditating? Was he a monk or something? A surfer monk who ate people when he caught them, as far as she knew. She decided right there to give up trying to understand anyone who lived in Adjacent, ever.

She felt suddenly very cold. Cold and empty. She wanted to get back to her own home and see her mother. To have a bath, sleep safely. To be a normal kid, cozy in a normal place. Not here.

She climbed down and found Tom. They were too exhausted to speak. They walked slowly back toward their homes, out in the open now, the only two kids out in the entire trailer park. They didn't notice or care.

The number of safe places in their lives was shrinking fast. Mrs. Clarke's trailer: occupied. Adjacent: under surveillance. School: swarming with cruel Poets.

Without a word, the two friends split and walked home.

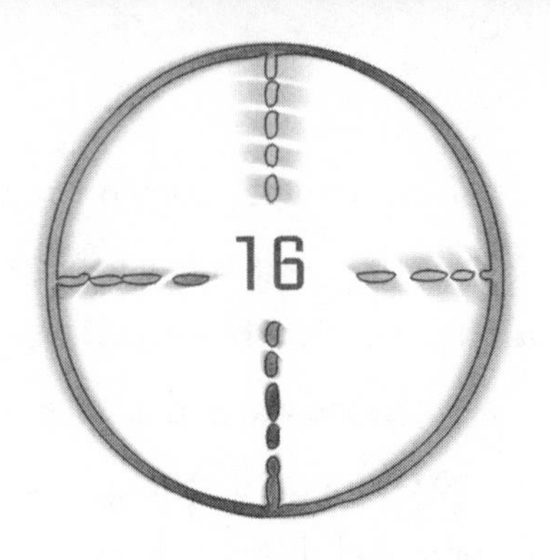

CIRCLES UNDERGROUND

ONE OF THE MOST TWISTED AND PATHETIC THINGS ABOUT living in this dusty armpit of a place was how much people cared about stupid little stuff, like what kind of shoes or belt buckle or cell phone you had. The sad part of it was that kids got most of this stuff by fishing around Trashmore. Cell phones especially: Every island kid had one that he or she had plucked from Trashmore, and of course none of the phones worked. Who were we gonna call, our senator?

But that didn't stop people from acting all special if they'd scored a slick phone, or pair of boots, or whatever it was. Everyone was trying to move up the ladder, just a step or two, even if they stepped on your head.

That ladder was everywhere, even on the school bus. Di and Tom were always the last students to get off, or close to last. Quartez got off first, Blasé second. Next came a stream of juniors and seniors, in some order that seemed to change but not much; and at the end were the stragglers, first-year middle school kids, and some eighth graders and freshmen who had few friends or defenders.

The schoolyard understood the order and immediately noted every exception to it. The morning after the Poets' ride into Adjacent the bus order changed, radically. No one missed it. Quartez came out first, as usual, looking so insanely hostile that kids stopped what they were doing.

Next were Ham and Thea, and they broke to the left and right and behind Quartez. Di and Tom stepped off next, into the cone of space between the older kids. Blasé brought up the rear. He had huge sunglasses on and was holding one of those feeling sticks that blind people use. Di heard some teacher say, "Oh my, what happened to Mr. Blasé's eyes."

Virgil and two other Poets stared them down without blinking. And did nothing. Quartez led the group, in tight formation, toward the entrance—and it was like the whole schoolyard stepped back to give them room.

"What's up with the freakin' security detail?" someone said. "Is that the Pope in there coming to visit TC or what?"

"No," another voice said. "That's Princess Di and Tom Jones."

"Who?"

Quartez shadowed Di the entire morning, even ditching out of some of his own classes early to check on her as she came out of each period.

In third period, Di had a Poet in her class, and Quartez lurked outside the door, giving him the death stare.

Blasé covered Tom, who wasn't sure he liked the extra attention. It meant that he couldn't disappear into the woodwork, or at least not disappear for long. Their bodyguards backed off finally at lunchtime, when Di found Tom sitting against the fence, close to one of his escape holes. He was trembling slightly, and she was turning her wrist and trying to take deep breaths.

"Hello," said a voice.

Di stifled a scream, and swung around. "Thea? What are you doing here?"

"Covering you, is what, while Rene D. and Pascal get a break. Listen. We need to talk. It looks like plant security is planning to shut down Adjacent. Completely."

"What, more than before?" Di said.

"They put barriers around the whole place. My mom called and told me about it. Everywhere but Far Corner, anyway. And they're telling people to lock themselves inside, that there's some kind of danger. It sounds, I don't know, it's like—it's totally crazy."

She looked intently at Di and Tom. "Look, I want in. I'm in, all the way."

“Really?” said Di, not sure if she was happy about it or not. Everyone seemed to be involved now, or wanted to be. “Tom?”

Tom was still staring off toward the sea, barely visible in the distance, still thinking about what Thea had said. Adjacent surrounded by barriers. Security swarming, closing people in.

One reason his father had liked Adjacent, Tom knew, was because it was wide open, close to the water, and out of the way. Off the grid, is what his dad sometimes said. Now it was some kind of target, back on the grid at the center of a bull's-eye. It struck Tom for the first time how alike he and his father were. Both preferred their private moments to stay private, not to be food for gossip at the bar or the store. Neither liked to hold himself out as the big papa expert, because they saw how easy it was to be wrong if you acted without thinking things through. Tom didn't know what the right word for all that was, but he knew that the words other people used—shy, timid, wallflower—were not correct.

Thea was still talking when he looked up. “Here's the thing,” she said. “You gotta go back down into the caves tonight. It's Wednesday, remember. High tide. A big high tide. Starts about nine-thirty. It's time to go back in.”

Tom shook his head. “Not right away. Not before figuring out the pi clue,” he said, and wrote down the clue for Thea on a piece of paper. “If we don't figure that out, we're not going to get much farther than we did before. Ask Ham; we need to find out which tunnels go from the y-pipe into the plant.”

"I just talked to him. He's going to meet us in Far Corner tonight. And there's a boy there, Oki Koulu—you know Oki, right?—he's got skills, he knows computers."

"The FC? Tonight?" Di said. "We'll get shredded by hounds out there."

"I talked to your mom, Lady Di. And I went by the Kebab Kart and talked to Mr. Muhammad too. The parents are all getting together later tonight to have some kind of town meeting to figure out what to do. It's a miracle, the adults are actually doing something. It will give us time to go back down."

Well, so much for that, Di thought. Other people were taking control. It was no longer just she and Tom.

"OK, OK, we'll be there," Di said.

The rest of the afternoon passed without incident and went surprisingly fast. The bus ride gave them far more time to think than usual. It took nearly an hour, because cars were lined up to the small causeway to get onto the island, and more still were waiting on the other side to leave. It got worse as they approached Adjacent. Security guards had surrounded the trailer park with makeshift wooden barriers, as Thea had said, and set up a checkpoint on the plant road.

Di stared out the window and saw plant workers, security people, Adjacent locals, more people coming and going than she had ever seen on the island at one time. Near the checkpoint, kids started to jump out of the bus and walk along the road, and the driver, not their usual one, didn't seem to mind. He looked like he wanted nothing more than to turn around and get away.

Di and Tom lost themselves easily in the crowd, ducked off the road, and hid for a while in the old outhouses. From there they moved behind a low ridge, and jogged in silence outside the barriers, to the bus graveyard, where they climbed up and into their favorite bus.

Through the windows looking south they could see the entire scene, the checkpoint, the plant, and all of Adjacent, which looked feeble from this view, behind the barriers. Guards were moving from trailer to trailer, talking to people or warning them. A voice broke their trance—a voice from a bullhorn.

"Ladies and gentlemen. Good citizens. A valuable piece of Folsom Energy property is missing, and we believe it has been stolen. Please be advised, we will be isolating the area."

They knew the voice instantly. Mr. Pink.

"Repeat: We will be isolating the area to conduct a thorough search beginning tomorrow. You are welcome to evacuate the island but will be submitted to a search."

"Evacuate?" said Di. "What the—what is he talking about? Evacuate all of Adjacent? Where are people going to go? Is it even legal?"

Di felt a rush of anger. Everyone was being so casual down there, taking orders from the plant. It was like people were being herded off a cliff. She couldn't believe that someone like Mr. Devlin or Mr. Rowan hadn't started shooting. She almost wished they would.

Tom had his hat down almost to his mouth now; the shrinking again. Both of them had prayed for something, anything to break the monotony of living in Adjacent. Now they wanted nothing more than to untwist the tape, to be in their trailers, bored, with nothing to worry about but homework. After what seemed like hours of grim silence, Di spoke up.

"Tom? You there? Hunt it down, remember? Be like a hound. Move and sniff. When you're moving, you're hunting. Let's get up and go find Oki and break this stupid pi clue."

It was the right call. Tom shook off his mood and took the lead, keeping low and far enough away from the barriers to be invisible in the dying twilight. He led them around the barriers that separated Adjacent from Far Corner, before cutting back over the road and into FC.

By the time they slipped in among the old trailers, the sky had gone dark, and off to their left and back they could see Adjacent swimming in the drunken light of flares set around the perimeter by security. Something had changed out here. Di sensed it immediately. The hounds stirred at their passing, and several jogged next to them in the dark, including a fat bloodhound and what looked like a long-nosed pug. No barking this time; the local hounds were providing an escort.

It was easy enough to find Oki's trailer. Voices could be heard out back. Thea's, Ham's, for sure, and maybe others, and there was a dim, flickering light from their midst, maybe a candle.

Suddenly eager for company, Di rushed toward the group. A sharp crunching sound stopped her dead—and she swallowed a shriek. A very fat man in a wheelchair surged out of the darkness and shoved a shotgun into her chest.

"Wherefor you goin', Frodo?" the man barked.

She made not a sound. Something wasn't right about the man. Sunglasses. He was wearing sunglasses. In the pitch darkness.

"Speak to me, Oki," the man said, cocking his head.

"It's OK, pop. They's with us," came a soft voice from near Thea and Ham. Di remembered the boy now: very dark, with big eyes, all knees and elbows. Homeschooled, like a lot of kids in Adjacent. "It's all right," the voice said to her. "He ain't shooting nobody. It's not even loaded."

"Thanks, Tonto," the old man said, swiveling in his chair. "How do you know it's not loaded?"

"He's also blind," the boy said. "Totally. So you can relax."

Di started to breathe again, and stared at the man with growing recognition. It was Lanny Hogben, or Hog, who had been a plant safety engineer or something and just dropped out of sight after he retired. How did Oki, who lived with his mom in FC, ever connect with this ancient, red-faced geezer? Di wondered. She shook her head. The old man was clearly teaching Oki things—and Hog knew a lot.

Di saw that Tom, behind her, was still shaken. And angry. He hated unpredictable lunatics, she knew, and it seemed that those were the only kind of people they were meeting.

"Uh, relax, OK. We'll try to," she said.

The two of them sat down on tires, joining the circle. In a few moments the old man appeared again, this time carrying a large bowl of popcorn and a six-pack of diet cream soda. Di was starving. She was torn between wanting to hug the man and to gobble the popcorn. She went for the corn, and the five of them passed the bowl around, eating great mouthfuls.

"All right," Thea said. "We got the clue that says 2 × 9 (π) and it could mean a lot of things, but we better solve it, and quickly. I've got some ideas, so let's get started." She pulled a folded envelope out of her back pocket, and a pencil. Di squirmed. Her wrist turned once, and she flushed: What was it? Not anxiety this time. Annoyance, that's what. She hated that Thea was taking over, talking about their clues, their project.

"Wait," she said. "Me and Tom found those clues, we found all of them. Mrs. Clarke left them for us, OK? We have ideas too."

"Who?" Thea said.

"Tom. Over there? He's sitting right there? Tom Jones? Well, we've been thinking about this longer than anyone, is what I'm saying."

"Fine," Thea said, cold now. "Let's hear what you got."

Di looked over at her friend. The dim light played across his face and she had no clue what he was thinking. She could feel the others' eyes on her, and the coolness in the air, the stillness of Far Corner, the sense of being on the edge of nowhere. She was no longer tired. She wasn't hungry. She was wide awake now, alert to every change in the air, every movement. She pulled a folded paper out of her own back pocket, and a pencil. She and Tom had made so many maps that they now carried around paper at all times.

"Well," she said. "First thing. If we can walk straight up the y-pipe and into the plant, that's what we're gonna do and forget all this clue stuff. You agree?"

The others practically roared, "*Heck yes!!*"

Di laughed. "But I got a feeling, you know, that she wouldn't have given us all these clues if it was that easy. We need a plan either way. So. Everyone has heard of pi r squared, the equation for the area of a circle. Let's start there."

The four of them leaned close over her drawing, which by now was familiar to all but Oki.

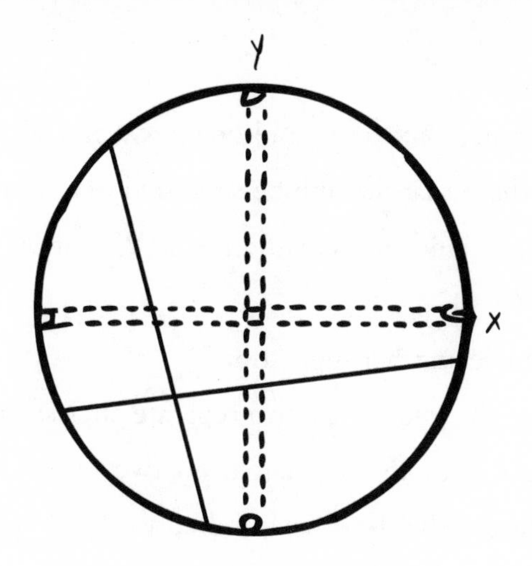

Several thoughts occurred to them. The clue read 2×9 (π).

If it referred to an area, then one possibility was that the area was $9 \times 2 = 18$. That is, $\pi r^2 = 18$.

Di pulled a small calculator from her pocket and calculated the radius. She used 3.14 for π:

$$3.14 \times r^2 = 18$$

$$r^2 = {}^{18}/_{3.14}$$

$$r = \sqrt{{}^{18}/_{3.14}}$$

$$r = 2.39$$

This was annoyingly complicated. But it was possible.

There was another possibility. The clue could refer to the circumference, not the area. The equation for the circumference, or the distance around a circle, was $2\pi r$. In that case the clue *was* a circumference: 2×9 (π) could be $2 \times \pi \times r$, where $r = 9$. Di reminded them that the numbers referred to hundreds of yards. So they might find tunnel entrances at 239 or 900 yards from the center (0, 0).

Tom made another suggestion.

"Maybe the two means two separate circles," he said. "And the nine refers to three squared. So two circles, each with a radius of three. That is, three hundred yards."

He drew another diagram:

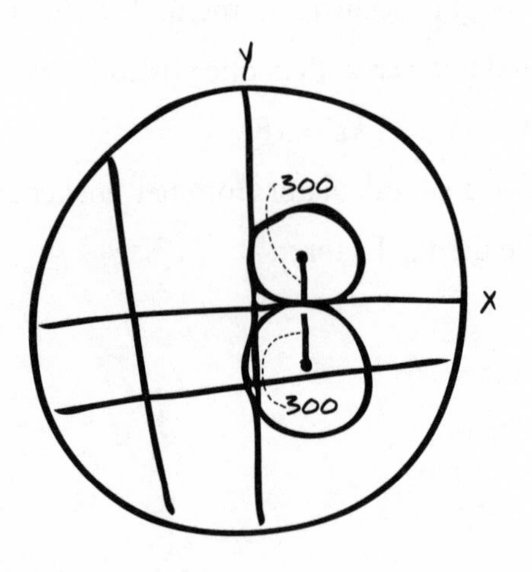

They stared at the drawing for some long moments. The variety of possible answers, and the strangeness of all the numbers themselves—pi was not exact, so that 2.39 looked strange—was making everyone restless.

"Well, we need to know where we're going before going in there," Ham said. "Look, maybe that symbol isn't pi at all."

Again they stared at the maps and equations, as if seeing them for the first time, starting all over.

"No. It is pi. It has to be pi." It was the boy, Oki. The first words he had spoken since the beginning.

Ham was annoyed. "Why does it *have* to be pi?"

"Well, because whoever left the clue drew a circle," said Oki. "That's not coincidence." He waited a moment and spoke again. "Them numbers we're getting, with all these decimal places, I don't like it either. But that's just, you know, what it is. I been using these computers in here a lot to calculate stuff and I hardly ever get exact numbers. Ever. I used to hate it but then I just got used to it. They're just numbers, is all."

He let that sink in, and started again, this time so softly the others had to lean in to hear him. "Mostly, though, I think this must be pi because I think pi is here. In this island. In this place."

"Oh yeah, it's whispering in the wind," Ham said. "Thank you, most holy one."

Everyone ignored him.

Oki looked down and drew a circle in the dirt.

"Pi's a number from the simplest thing there is, and still it can't be calculated exactly. It's like it outsmarted all the biggest mathematicians, and made supercomputers crash, seriously. No one knows what pi's gonna do next."

"It seems like some kinda magic number," said Di. "You know?"

"Aargh, *no*!" a thick voice coughed out. It was the old man,

Hog, rattling to life. "Ain't no such thing as magic out here, Princess Leia. None. If Adjacent hasn't taught you that, then you're beyond learnin'."

Di, stung, was speechless; the group went quiet as well.

Tom felt a tingle in his lower back and looked up into the sky, as if he might find some guidance there. A broken quilt of dark flannel clouds ran out to infinity over the open sea. His mind braided the map of the island into the clouds: The larger circle, with a radius of 900 . . . then the smaller ones, with radii 300 and 239. He was surprised when the figures, which glowed in his head with a white-sand color, dissolved without carrying him off into one of his daydreams.

"Listen," Ham said, almost hissing the words, "I'm not going back down there unless we know exactly which passage we're taking."

Oki shook his head. "We don't have to know for sure." That quiet voice; the boy was so still, tucked into a squat with his head practically resting on his knees. "We have enough information. It's not like there are going to be fifty circle tunnels down there. We can use the guesses we have, try every single one and see what matches."

"Trial and error," Thea said.

"Brute force," Oki said.

He explained further. The clue had three solutions that made sense. And there were five of them. If in fact there were three openings leading from the y-pipe toward the plant and matching those locations, then one person could stay behind and the others could take one opening each, to save time, and there would be one person to spare. Ham could stay behind, he suggested.

"That means if your brain starts capsizing down there, you can haul ass back out through the Trashmore entrance," Thea said. "But you best yell in at us and tell us first."

"Uh-huh . . . OK. And which way do you go if the y-pipe starts shooting water?" Ham said.

"Forward," Tom said. "Forward. To get back we'll just have to time it and rush across the y-pipe. Or wait."

Ham squinted at Tom for a second or two, as if he'd only just noticed he was there.

"One problem, though," Di said, looking over at Oki. "How do we know we're in a circle tunnel, and what the radius is? You haven't been down there. You have no idea how lost you feel. You can't see anything and you can't tell which way is which."

She looked over at Tom for support and saw that he was smiling. He was holding up a compass.

"I'll show you how you tell," he said. "You watch."

THE CONTROL ROOM

THIS IS NOT A HUGE DISCOVERY OR ANYTHING, BUT, honestly, some old people are just plain gnarly, and there's nothing you can do about it. They kind of bark at you, and squint at you like you're always doing something wrong, and you don't want to go too close because they stink and have some egg-looking stuff on their lips, or whatever. But here's the thing about geezers. If one of those suckers is on your side—if the goat is actually pulling for you, which can happen—then you don't mind the stale smell so much, or that they have moles with hair sprouting out.

Hog was starting to seem like that, Di thought. The old man brought them a few supplies. A can of cream soda each. A few plastic bags of BBQ sunflower seeds. Water. Most important, two small flashlights.

“Thank you, sir,” Thea said.

He motioned for her to come near and handed her an ancient hunting knife. “Don’t let Tin Tin there near this,” he said, tipping his head toward Oki. The boy rolled his eyes.

“And don’t get in your own way,” the man said. “The lights are out down there, that’s all. Everything else, your ears, your nose, still work fine. Better than you think. You’ll get used to it fast, you’ll see.”

He paused. “And you best bring back this boy alive, or I will find some ammunition.”

Thea looked at the others, and Ham shrugged. “All right, suckers, let’s move out,” he said. Tom nodded to Di, and the group turned and followed her.

Di knew Tom was dying to explain his solution using the compass—because he wanted to beat Oki to it.

Before they set out, she sat down with pen and paper and tried to figure it out herself. It was the only way she could keep her mind off of what was coming. She worried about Mrs. Clarke. She worried more about her mother and what would happen if they had to move. She dared not think about herself, and the long night ahead of her, crawling around like an ant underground.

She tried some Mrs. Clarke advice. Simplify. Take the simplest version of the problem and solve that. Then try the harder ones.

She assumed that the correct tunnel was a circle with a

radius of nine—meaning nine hundred yards—with its center at (0, 0).

She pictured that in her mind. Really pictured it. She saw immediately that if she walked around that circle far enough, well, she would hit the x-axis, the x-pipe.

But how many yards until she would hit it? Even bouncing along toward Trashmore she could see that that was easy: exactly one quarter of the circle.

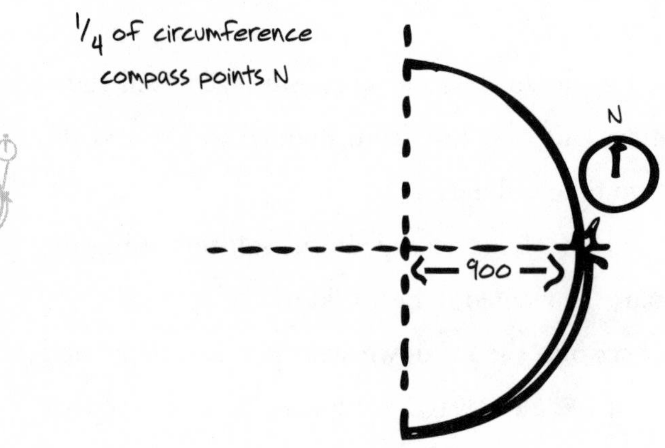

The distance was one quarter around the circumference. She could see the circle in her head, with one quarter of its outline colored blood red. The circumference was ($2\pi r$), so a quarter of that was $\frac{1}{4} \times 2\pi r$. She used her calculator, and took π as 3.14 to simplify. So, $\frac{1}{4} \times (2 \times 3.14 \times 900)$.

About one thousand four hundred and thirteen yards.

She wouldn't need the compass for that: She'd know she had

it because she would hit the x-pipe. If she did have a compass, though, it would be pointing directly north as soon as she arrived at the x-pipe. And then she saw it and understood.

No matter how big or small the circle was, you could calculate the number of paces it took to get to where you were walking directly north. Think about it. You walked that number of paces—yards—and if the compass was directly at N when you got there, then you almost certainly had a circular tunnel. It also worked for the circles Tom described, using half the circumference.

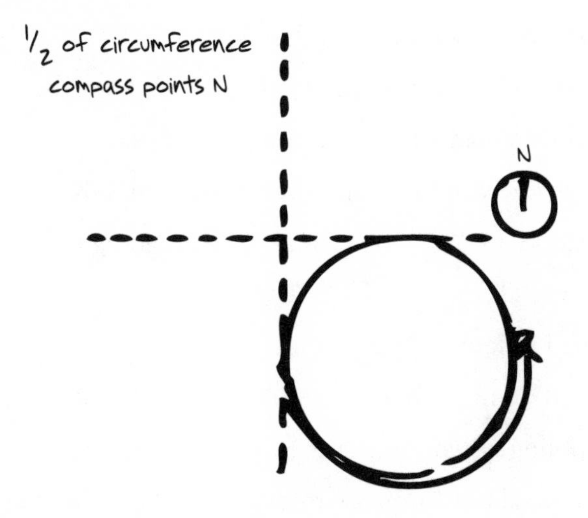

Di stood up. "Let's move."

They arrived at the abandoned fridges and plunged through. Single file they went, under Trashmore, flashlights drawn, Tom first, then Thea, Di, Oki, and Ham. The place didn't stink as much as during the day but it was crawling with bugs, rodents, and who knew what. The whole mountain seemed so teeming with life, eating itself from the inside, and it was best to move fast and not look too closely. Once all five were down in the small underground room, Di shone her flashlight on their faces.

She caught Ham trying to sneak the sunflower seeds out of Thea's pack. "Get out, you rat," Thea said.

"What? I can't snack?" Ham said. He turned toward Oki, who was crouching again, showing Tom something about the compass. "Hey, big man, trade flashlights with me. This one's perfect for you."

"If it's so great, you keep it," Oki said.

"OK, OK," Di said. She could tell by the look on Tom's face that he knew she had solved the compass problem. She didn't know how he knew but he did. "Everybody stop, OK?"

"So," said Ham. "Tell us again how this is going to happen, Commandante Di."

Di turned to look at Thea. "Tide report."

"It should be high enough in about thirty minutes to shut down the cooling system," she said. "Once the pipe stops flushing we should have about forty-five minutes, maybe an hour at the most. It's nine thirty on the spot right now. Everyone, coordinate your watches."

No one else had one but they all stared at their wrists anyway.

"All right," said Di. "Thirty minutes is about enough time to get us to the y-pipe, if we hurry. Once we get there Tom—Tom, Tom Jones, OK?—he will take Oki and Thea will come with me. We'll split up to see which of the tunnels could be the right circle tunnel. Ham, you'll stay back in the y-pipe."

Ham puffed his chest and saluted dramatically. The others nodded and said, "OK."

Di and Tom set the pace through the tunnels, swift but not reckless. The tunnels were crumbling, the floors jagged in places, and one sprained ankle would ruin the whole project, probably for good. At the open x-pipe, Di dropped back behind Thea. The bigger girl would need someone to talk her through the narrow section; everyone did.

Soon they were on their bellies, inching forward on their elbows. Tom was whispering advice to Oki up ahead, and Ham was scratching along in the middle.

"It gets very, very tight coming up here. OK, Thea? Very tight."

"OK."

"At the end of this section it's going to look bad but it's not, really." She told her about the puddle. Di could tell by Thea's breathing that she was very close to panic. Up in front, Tom was having similar problems with Oki. But at least Oki was small; he wasn't being squeezed as badly as the others. Di continued her patter to Thea while staring at the older girl's shoes.

"Don't worry, you'll fit . . . I fit, and I'm fat . . . I mean, I'm fat and not very fit, you know what I mean . . . hey, this is as narrow as it gets, honestly, this is it. Through the puddle and we're out."

Dead-black darkness, the far-off sound of dripping water, the smell of cold stone earth: the certainty that if this rock shifted a single inch there would be no escape. Your lungs could barely expand to get air. Was there enough air? Was it running out? Di knew these thoughts must be strangling Thea.

"Hey, Thea, did you ever notice that Ham is trying to grow a beard or a something? Like on his chin and lips, only it's so light you can't see it? I think he has more hair on his ears . . . seriously, he's like an old man that way—"

"Hey, shut it, Babar!" Ham yelled from up ahead. "I'm surprised your butt even fits through there."

"Seriously," Di continued, to Thea. "He's got bushes growing out back there—"

"OK!" Ham yelled. "I'm at the puddle. I'm going under. If I die, dump my body in Mrs. Perkins's lame science class, back by the windows. Eighth graders can dissect me." Di heard a soft splash ahead, and thrashing as Ham pulled himself through. This was it. She knew that whatever Thea was feeling now would only get worse when she saw the water up ahead. The only way through it was to slow down, slow down time. Panic would kill her down here.

"OK, Thea? Stop for a second. Breathe. That's all. Just do

that. You could fall asleep right here and be fine for hours. Seriously, you could. Stare at the rock for a second. Right in front of your face. What kind of rock do you think that is? You took earth science, right? Limestone? Just stare at it, OK?"

"OK," came the answer, in a small voice.

"Breathe. That's all you're doing. We're having a conversation here, is all . . . OK. Just in front of you is a small, watery area. The puddle I told you about. You have to roll over so you're on your back . . . are you there?"

"I can see it. Oh. Di, I can't. I can't do it, oh no."

"You can see it: Good. That's the way out. It looks bad but isn't. It's one of those, what do you call it?—optical illusions. Seriously, it is."

Di laughed a little to sound natural. And it did, sort of.

"Thea, you have to turn over, squeeze your arms forward. You hold your breath for a second. Drop down. And pull yourself down under and around, through the puddle, to the other side. You understand? It's just a few feet deep and slippery, which is good, you'll kind of slip down in there, and feel up with your hands to pull yourself up. And that's that, there's more room on the other side . . . but just do the same thing you're doing now: stare at the stone, go slow . . . slow . . . you heard me, right? Slow?"

"Di, I'm—"

"Say 'slow,' one time."

"Slow."

"Again"

"Slow."

"OK. One, two, three," Di said, and she heard the splash, louder this time, and then quiet, then desperate sounds, and nothing again. The shoes had disappeared completely through the puddle. Thea had to be through. Huge relief.

Di ducked her head under. It was colder than last time, enough to take half her breath. She groped up on the other side, found a ledge on the facing rock, and eased herself through.

Tom picked up the pace again on the other side, then slowed as he approached the y-pipe. He was taking no chances with the water, even though no more than fifteen minutes had passed since they started, according to Thea's watch.

When the pipe was active, the water blasts came fifteen to twenty seconds apart. That first trip into the y-pipe, Di realized, had been lucky: It had been off, and was just turning on when they climbed out. Tom stopped the group just short of the pipe and waited twenty seconds. Thirty seconds. Forty. Nothing.

The pipe was off.

The first thing they noticed when they climbed into the pipe was the light, a bluish glow, seemingly coming out of the pipe walls, enough that they could switch off the flashlights.

"What is this, are we getting nuked right now, is that what this is?" Ham said. "I think I feel my balls shriveling."

"Will you *shut* it for once?" Thea said.

Ham made a sucking sound and smiled. Di and Tom studied the pipe walls and found tiny light sources embedded behind a clear outer layer. Thea said the lights were probably necessary, so that the pipe could be maintained at night. "You'd have to be able to keep this clear and running, and fix things at any hour."

Suddenly, everyone was a cooling pipe expert, Di thought. She was simply glad to have some light. She pulled out the map. Tom had traced out the three most likely circle tunnels. First he had drawn one with a radius of 239 yards, and one with a radius of 900 yards:

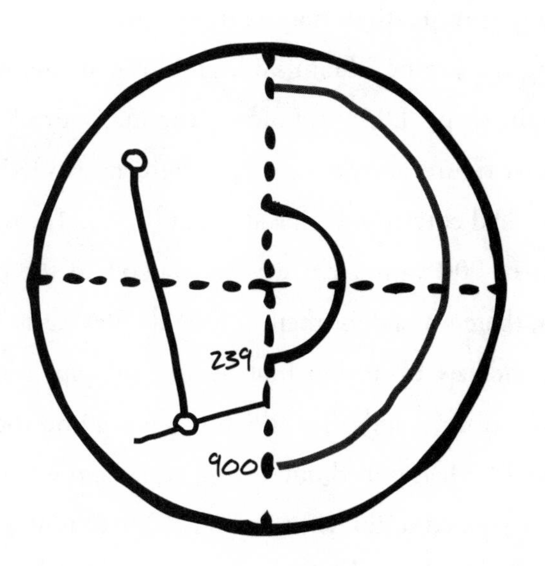

Tom had then sketched out his own idea, two circles, each with a radius of 300 yards:

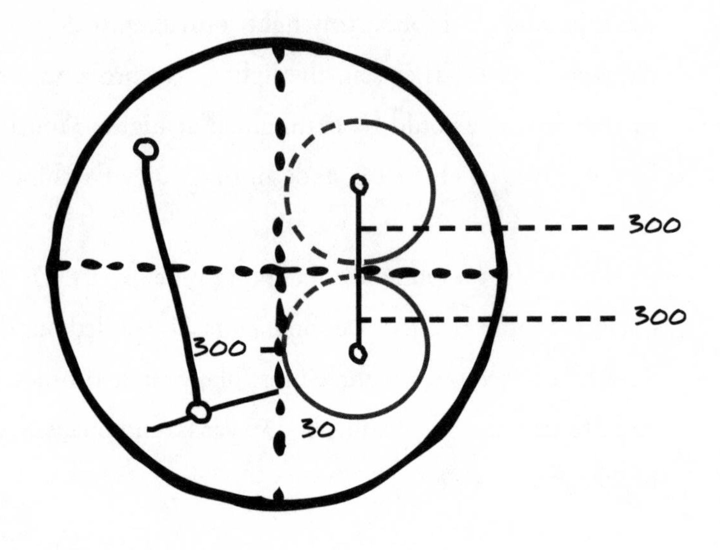

"Hey, gimme that map, I'm the one supposed to be covering the y-pipe," Ham said, grabbing at the paper.

"Wait, stop," Di said, holding the map out of his reach. "Let's just figure out where we are right now, OK?"

They had entered the pipe at about (0, -6). The tunnel with a radius of 900 yards, if it existed, was off to the right. Sure enough, there was a door there at roughly 900 yards. Di looked around and saw Ham slouching against the pipe wall, playing imaginary drums, and Thea and Tom staring into the throat of the pipe. Oki had pulled out a small stone and was rubbing it, which he seemed to do when nervous, Di had noticed.

She asked Oki to check out the door at the 900-yard mark.

Oki slipped into it, and came back out. He shrugged. "Could be. We can't count it out."

"OK, stay there," Di said. "Ham, you head down to the two-hundred-thirty-nine-yard mark and see what's there. Thea, you count down to the three hundred point and check that; and then run back, OK?"

"I can't see the map? Whaddup with that? I'm the y-pipe guy, remember?" said Ham. Di let him look at it, and he passed it to Thea, who handed it back to Di.

The two older kids then took off, half-stepping into the blue light, looking as goofy as those power walkers Di had seen on TV. They were back in minutes. Ham had found nothing at the 239-yard mark. No tunnel entrance.

"Scratch it," he said, and began playing an imaginary keyboard.

At a point about 300 yards from (0, 0), Thea had found a door, and a looping pathway behind it.

"That could be the one; you can see it goes in for a ways," said Thea. She was doing stretches, as if preparing for an athletic event. Oki still had his stone and Tom was kind of bobbing his head to some private rhythm; he was having fun, Di knew.

"Good, we're down to two tunnels," Di said. "Does everyone see that on the map?" She held the map up for them, with the tunnel at 239 yards crossed out. Ham made another lunge at the paper, and Di moved it just out of reach.

“Harsh me severely,” Ham said. “When do I get that thing?”

“Now,” Di said. “Here.”

She had Tom and Oki explore the bigger tunnel and she went with Thea to explore the other one. Each pair had a compass and flashlight.

The tunnel that Thea had found 300 yards from dead center was narrow but tall enough in most places to stand.

Di had an odd sensation when she entered that she was curving away from the x-axis, not toward it. She decided to let the numbers decide. If this was a circle, with its center at (0, 0) and with a radius of 300, then they should hit the x-pipe and be facing directly north at the same time. That would have to happen after going a quarter of the way around.

Di had made the calculation and written it on her hand: $\frac{1}{4} \times (2\pi r)$, or $\frac{1}{4} \times 2 \times 3.14 \times 300 \approx 470$ paces.

It didn’t happen.

After 460 paces she felt no closer to the x-pipe, and the compass said they were facing directly east. She double-checked it. Thea held her place while Di walked up and back with the compass, making sure it was working and not just stuck on east. She shook it too. Same result: east. Her instincts had been right on; the tunnel did not arc directly toward the x-pipe.

“Maybe it’s not a circle at all,” Thea said.

"No, I think it is, but obviously not one that goes around zero zero. Think about it. We curved away from the x-axis and now we're starting to move back toward it. Remember the two circles Tom talked about?"

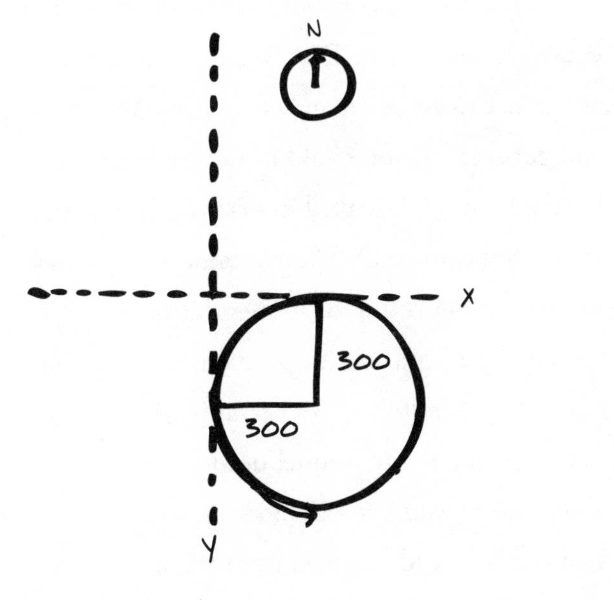

Thea stretched her arms behind her head, rolled her shoulders, her wrists; the girl had some kind of weird martial-arts-looking routine she was always going through. "Yeah, it must be," Thea said. "Those were the two circle tunnels, one that went from y-axis to x-axis, and the other under the plant?"

"Exactly," said Di. The two of them had an urge to run forward, toward the positive x-axis. They resisted, turned, and scrambled back, as fast as they could.

"It's a circle, it's pretty much a circle all right," Thea said to Ham when they got back to the y-pipe.

She was out of breath, Di noticed, and not so cold and commanding as usual. Thea had that look—wired, flushed, wide-eyed but patient, observant—the tunnel look: Exploring a cave is one thing, Di thought. But it was something else altogether to go down and stay down. Your eyes opened wider, you got smaller, you could feel every breath. Like scuba diving in stone. The chill soaked under your skin and stayed there and after a while it was OK. You became a lizard, basically. You were not the person you were above ground.

Oki and Tom had to pace out a quarter of a much larger circle, $\frac{1}{4} \times (2\pi 900) \approx 1{,}413$ yards or so for their circle. They never got there. The tunnel dead-ended into a pile of rock at about 1,000 yards. It was blocked, with no way through. They scurried back and emerged from the tunnel a few minutes after Di and Thea had.

"Que pasa, señores?" said Ham, who was now lying in the base of the y-pipe, as if he were in his hammock.

"What're you doing, napping?" said Tom "We're running out of time, c'mon."

"I think better when I'm relaxed, is what," Ham said.

"Well, this tunnel is totally blocked. Think about that," Tom said.

"That's it then," Di said. "Two circles, each radius three

hundred paces. That's what the evidence so far tells us." It was the first time she'd used the word "evidence" and she thought it came out OK. "So, one circle goes to the x-axis pipe and the other into the plant. Like Tom said. Exactly like he predicted. Let's go." It sounded good. But none of them believed it. And Di was as surprised as any of them when, after about ten minutes of slogging in the dark, she pushed open a door and there it was: the positive side of the x-axis pipe.

"Oh brother, look at this," Di said.

It was a mirror of the Mount Trashmore side of the pipe. The same width, the same smell of the sea, the feel of being abandoned, apparent even now, in the dark. No embedded safety lights here, only a faint pale glow coming from the mouth of the pipe, which opened high in the cliff face, revealing a circle of night sky, flecked with stars. The biggest difference was the noise. A great chugging hum that seemed to be coming from inside the rock on the other side of the pipe. They were close.

"So what's this place look like?" said Oki.

Nobody answered.

"Wait, uh-oh, you have no idea what we're looking for?" he said.

Ideas they had, Di thought. Mrs. Clarke was leading them into the plant to stop something, Di was almost certain now, and that meant they would find either another message, an ally, or maybe Mrs. Clarke herself inside. Still, Di felt they were missing something: Mrs. Clarke was usually clear in explaining things. Did she leave them something they hadn't found? Oki was right: By now someone should know exactly what the mission was. Di asked for the time, to change the subject.

"About twenty minutes have passed. We have about forty minutes left. Max," Thea said. The second opening was exactly where their map had it, just across from the one they had left:

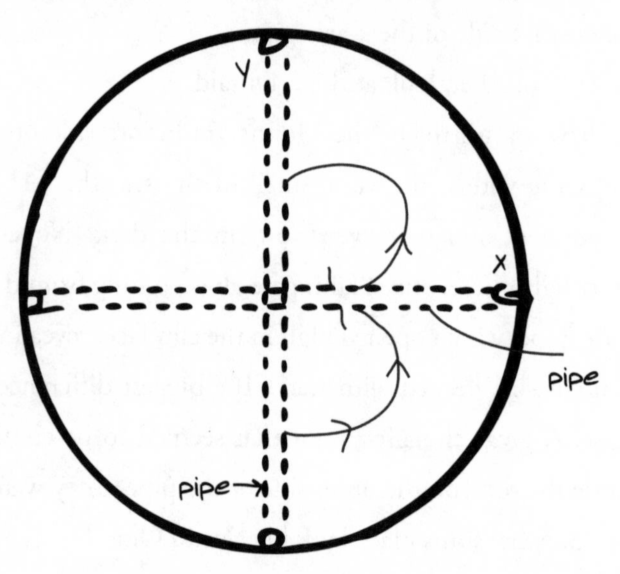

Tom took the lead and picked up the pace: This tunnel was in better shape. No collapsed sections, the ceiling was plenty high, and the footing was good. It sloped down too, Di noticed; they were going deeper in. They rounded a bend and hit a wall. The machine noise was clearly coming from just on the other side.

Tom played his flashlight over the wall and then passed his hand over it. “Plywood,” he said. He pushed at the wood and it immediately swung open. He slipped through the crack and the others followed. One by one they squeezed past a massive humming black box, rounded the corner, and stopped again.

“Oh brother,” Di said. They stood at the edge of a giant opening. A massive room, larger by far than any interior space they had ever seen or imagined. A few unseen bulbs cast a grayish light over an underground universe of steel. Pipes like climbing vines up the walls. More running across the ceiling, thirty feet in the air at least, forming a great hanging maze of metal. Off in the middle distance, as if floating in the ghostly light, were several metal staircases rising into the darkness. It appeared there were several floors, or levels, that the stairs passed through, like metal cages. The floor where they stood was itself a thick metal grate, and they could feel more than see at least two giant generators of some kind beneath the floor. This was the source of the deep chugging sound.

A sign posted on a huge steel pillar near them read, ZERO LEVEL. BLACK GANG AND EXECUTIVE ONLY. An industrial acid tang bit at their nostrils.

“Uh, is it just me, or are we here?” Di said.

“Zero Level. That’s too raw,” Ham said.

Di glanced over at Tom and he nodded his cap slightly. She wondered if he had the strange sensation she did: A tingling in her back and neck that made her stand up straight and smile slightly. She'd had the feeling once before and couldn't quite place it.

"What now, Princess?" Ham said.

She saw nothing moving in the place. It was late at night, maybe ten thirty, and it didn't look like many people worked down here even during the day. Di was worried about the time: Forty minutes left now, she thought, at most. She knew that it might be possible to scramble across the negative y-pipe between blasts of water but no one wanted to risk that. She knew too that the others expected her and Tom to have a plan. If only. She had a sudden thought.

"Look, most of the light is coming from there, in the center," she said. "Let's split up and meet over there. Ham, you move along this wall. Thea, you take that wall. Oki, Tom and I will divide up the middle and see what's here."

She paused. "We're looking for—a computer." She didn't know exactly why she thought of that. Maybe because she knew it might stop Oki, who was a computer head, from asking so many questions. Or maybe just because it sounded good.

Tom sensed something was off. He looked up from under his cap and was about to speak, but Oki cut him off.

"Yeah, I thought that's what it was, that makes sense," he said.

Thea immediately backed him up. "That has to be where we start, absolutely."

So it was decided. They fanned out across the expansive floor and moved forward, looking for a computer, or anything else that could be useful.

Zero Level was a land of giants. Two rows of thirty-foot-tall upright cylinders, encased in metal. And elongated blocks, rectangular humming machines about five feet tall, the same as the one in front of the entrance to the tunnels. These too had sheer steel sides and were hot to the touch.

The whole place was filled with machine heat and noise. At least no one would hear them down here, Di thought. Below the metal-grate floor were monstrous machines of some kind—the power source itself, maybe—and there were manholes with vertical ladders going down. Tom barely sidestepped one and said a quick prayer that he'd seen it. A fall down below the grate was almost certainly the end. It looked like the hole went to the center of the earth.

Ham was not so lucky. He noticed a manhole the moment that his right foot dropped below the floor, and down he went, with a loud clang—his giant belt buckle had caught on the lip of the hole.

He yelled, "Heeey!!" and somehow Di heard it above the noise.

She veered over and helped pull him up. The two crouched there for a moment, to recover.

Soon the five of them had gathered together again where the light pooled, under the metal staircase. The light was coming from way up, near the ceiling, and it was bright up there, outlining what looked like a door with a glass panel.

"OK, I don't really want to ask, but how much time do we have left?" said Di.

Thea looked at her watch. "Twenty minutes. Maybe thirty, at the most. But we gotta go up. We came too far. I'm not turning back, not now, that's for sure."

The others weren't so certain. Di was starting to get that familiar ache in her stomach, her wrist was twitching, and she was mumbling to herself: Track the problem. Write down what you know.

"Follow the problem," she said, out loud.

"That's what I'm talking about," Thea said.

Up they went, jogging up the steel stairs like boot camp marines. It felt for a moment like a gym class exercise, not an attempt to break into Folsom Energy, *the* Folsom Energy, one of the biggest nuclear plants in the country. The door at the top of the stairs erased any doubts of where they were. On the other side of the thick glass was a brightly lit control center of some kind, complete with chairs on wheels and a bank of colorful knobs and buttons and lights. Pressure dials, coolant level readings, output and input levers. All labeled, clearly visible. A sign over one console read, COMPONENTS, CAPACITY. But where were all the people?

"I'll go in, Lady Di," said Ham. "All we need is to find one computer, right?"

"Uh, right," Di said.

"Say no more," Ham said, and pushed through the door and strolled right in as though he owned the place.

The others gasped, jostled for viewing space, saw him disappear around a corner. It was no longer possible to claim, if caught, that they had wandered by mistake into the plant. Now they were trespassing. Tom was the first to notice an open soda can and bag of chips near one of the consoles. Someone was working! If that person returned with Ham loose in there, it was over.

"Let's step back a little. We can be seen!" Tom whispered.

They drew back just in time, as the door swept open. Thea turned to escape, hit the railing, and almost went over.

"Boo!"

It was Ham. Thea almost reached over and slapped his head. "Why don't you just knock us all to the floor next time, you clown," she said.

"Look," Ham said. "Just around the corner, there's a meeting room. Full. They're talking in there. Get in here now and let's listen. The door is open. Maybe we can hear something, seriously. And a bathroom down the hall, if you need to hide. C'mon."

Di felt her heartbeat in her temples. She hadn't known what to expect and this was getting far too serious too quickly. Not to mention that they had only about twenty minutes before their escape was cut off. *Maybe* twenty minutes. If you're moving you're hunting, she said, almost out loud.

“OK,” she said. “Ham, take the door. Tom, do a quick circle of the room, to see if there’s anything we can use. Me and Thea and Oki will go listen.” She pushed into the room, fully expecting to be instantly busted, and turned the corner, feeling a tremendous weight in her legs. One foot in front of the other, she thought. It was just like Ham said: An open door, spilling out a fluorescent glow, a corner room. A narrow corridor running off to the right. She held her wrist so it wouldn’t turn and crack: This was real.

She took a position next to the open door, and glanced over her shoulder; Thea and Oki were right there, she could feel their warmth. Oki was silently breathing on his lucky stone. Tom was moving like a cat around the consoles, looking for a computer terminal; he was doing what looked like air karate moves, Di saw.

Ham was crouching by the door, looking blissful. He had found a staple gun and was holding it like a weapon.

Di leaned in close to the door and knew immediately that this was no ordinary conversation. Three, four, maybe five voices, one female. One, maybe two familiar.

Who?

Mr. Pink: no mistaking him. And he was pleading with someone, for what? She could not make it out. But: Mr. Pink had a boss.

Di felt suddenly light-headed. This was too much. Here she was, fifteen feet from valuable information, and she couldn’t make out anything but random words. “Stimulation” or "simulation" was one; another was "flushrive" or something, and whatever that was, it was very important. It was something they wanted but didn't have, Di sensed.

She leaned in closer.

A sweaty silence throbbed in the meeting room now; someone sighed.

Then a chair scratched the floor, someone said, "Wait!" and Di pulled back. She raised a hand signal, and the five of them scattered.

Ham ducked back through the door to the stairs, and slid down to a lower landing. Tom took two long steps and slid under a desk back where he had been exploring. Di, Thea, and Oki turned and scrambled for the bathroom—the women's room. It crossed Di's mind that this doomed caper had started in an outhouse and now would probably end in an underground women's room.

Did they see the door close? No time to think—the small room had a sink, two stalls, and in the corner a chemical shower with a black door—and in they went, practically having to bear-hug each other, Thea pulling the door shut.

"I swear something moved out here. Lydia, check the downstairs door. Pincus, you take the bathrooms. Let's just make sure." Mr. Pink's real name was actually Mr. Pincus: How perfect, Di thought. Did anyone else call him Mr. Pink? Mr. Pink-ass probably.

Bizarre what traveled through your mind when you were

about to be busted inside a nuclear plant. Di held her breath and prayed. She heard Mr. Pink-ass's shoes click clack down the corridor and toward the bathroom.

Now the bathroom door was opening, the shoes were so close but—where?—not right here. He was in the men's room next door. Footsteps moving away. He hadn't even looked in the women's room! Hard to be sure, but it seemed after a few minutes that the adults had gone back into the meeting room, and again were talking. Di, Tom, and the others had only one thing on their minds: bail. They waited ten beats, twenty, twenty-five— the conversation in the meeting room now had some rhythm—and then made a move for the door.

Thea got there first, crouching low, and looking back for the other three. She slipped through and held it open. Di, Tom, and Oki hurried like spooked mice on all fours.

All three heard an alarmed voice yell, "Hey! Dammit!"

Down the stairs they went, almost tumbling, one landing, two, and almost to the floor when the door swung open. They followed Ham, who ducked toward the back wall where there was no light. At least two people were now clanging down the stairs, and the lights were coming on: row by row overhead, from the far side of the great Zero Level vault. They ran just ahead of the lights, all except for Di, the slowest, who felt the lights on her back and her orange hair ablaze. Her cover was blown, it had to be.

Tom took the lead now, pushing into the tunnel and up the slope, feeling the sides with outstretched hands. He didn't dare use his flashlight.

They moved back through the circular tunnel—Tom counting paces the whole way, by habit—and poured out into the x-pipe. Thea stared at her watch and yelled, "Go go go go, we have only a few minutes!"

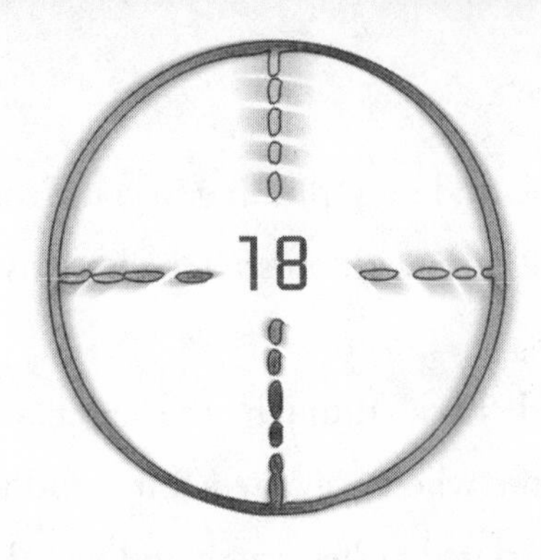

THE CIRCUMFERENCE

THEY RAN FOR THEIR LIVES. SCRATCHED THEIR WAY through the circular tunnel with their arms, palms, and forearms as much as their legs. When it counted most their bodies remembered the way, turning when the tunnel walls narrowed, ducking when the rock ceiling jutted low.

Di and Tom in particular seemed to move by instinct now, as quickly as any cave-dwelling animals. It wasn't enough. Tom heard the rumble of the water, stopped himself some twenty yards short of the y-pipe, before being hit with stinging spray. The chain of kids collapsed back on itself in a scratching, soaking panic. The hot water felt like acid against their cooled skin.

"Thea! Thea!" Di screamed over the thunder. "Turn and get us out!" Thea dragged herself up, turned, pulled Di behind her, who pulled on Oki, and slowly the train reversed itself, stumbling at first, then picking up speed. They tumbled hard into the x-pipe and followed Thea out toward the mouth on the east side of the island. She ran to the very edge, and dropped to her knees. She peered out, desperately looking for something.

"C'mon, come on—yes! OK. Tom, you first. See that ledge running to the right from the mouth of the pipe?"

Many ledges ran around the outside of the island, like bulges of frosting between layers on a cake. One running past the pipe was prominent enough to hold on to.

"Hold on to the ledge and use your feet against the wall. It's easier than you think. Just don't look down," she said. "There's footholds all along here; you'll see."

Tom hesitated, then swung out onto the cliff and out of sight.

"No! He's gonna fall—Tom!" Di was shaking and lunged toward the opening.

"You're next," Thea said. The rock cliffs of the island tapered out on this side, and the rock face was knotted and pocked by millions of years of wind and water. Thea was right: footholds everywhere. And there was Tom, Di saw, propped on the cliff wall, with his fingers locked into the ledge.

"It's not hard, c'mon!" he yelled over the wind. She swung out and held on. The sudden rush of open air and sea spray brought a kind of tingling, floating strength. The tunnels, as dark and tiring as they were, always made her feel wild and alive once she was back above ground. Thea was the last one out. She thought she had seen something moving in the pipe behind her, another person, but couldn't be sure.

They pressed forward along the wall, back toward the Point. They made good progress for a while, but it couldn't last. Di's fingers would start to bleed soon; so would the others'. She finally spoke up: "So, uh, exactly where are we going, Thea? Are we close to stopping?"

"The ledge is widening, slightly. You see it?" Thea said. Keep going, another twenty or thirty yards, and it'll be wide enough to climb up and sit on. There's a cave up there. We can rest," she said.

The word "rest" lent an angry determination to their movements. Several minutes later, their fingers raw, they saw the crevice open up like a smile above them. From the next high foothold Tom pushed himself up and rolled in. Di joined him.

She heard grunts and gasps behind her as the others followed. She turned to make sure: They were all there, breathing heavily, their breath fogging in the cool darkness. And there they lay for a long while, staring out into the vast oil drum of the eastern sky, liquid black with a spray of starlight. The ocean swell had dropped, and a breeze massaged the rock face, humming through the opening and tingling on their necks. A lonely organ-note moan of a ship came from the port off to their left. A sense of hopeless solitude made the skin on Di's arms crawl. What now?

Cold and dark and nobody knows where you are. This is what it must be like, she thought, to be lost at sea.

Tom, seated with his feet dangling over the edge, had something like the opposite sensation. A long time lost at sea in his own head, he now saw in this group a place to land. He was not entirely comfortable with any one of them, except for Di, and wasn't sure what they really thought of him, if anything. But they knew his name, and they listened to what he said, and for a second Tom wondered if that was all a group of friends really was. He had no idea.

Through the dark he could see Di, propped on one elbow, Oki in his crouch, Ham and Thea flat on their stomachs, peering out over the water. The whole earth seemed to be resting with them, tilting on its axis, breathing with their fogged breath through the crooked mouth of the island, seeing the sea and sky with their eyes.

Di gasped, and Tom banged his head on the rock ledge, when a giant sea bird of some kind swept in very close and landed with a pounding of wings on a perch just below them. Clicking, breathing bird sounds came from under where they lay.

"Hah, look, it's got babies in there," Ham whispered, pointing to the nest. Di peeked over the lip of the rock and saw the nest. The salt-air smell out there and the color—the sky was a dome of polished black cherry—were so strong that Di wondered if this was what it was like being a baby bird, with big eyes and everything so new, so strange.

Oki eventually broke the spell. “I don’t know if any of yous are planning to spend the rest of your lives here, but I tell you what. Lady Di and Tom, y’all best figure out exactly what our mission is supposed to be, otherwise we just did a whole lot of scary creeping around for nothing.” A big speech for Oki, and from his crouch he gave Di his big-eyed stare.

“OK, OK, I don’t know exactly, I’m not a nuclear genius with X-ray vision or anything,” Di said. She sat up and dangled her feet over the edge, next to Tom, looking back at the other three. “My theory, and I told this to Tom, is that Mrs. Clarke wants us to stop the plant people from doing something. It must be something bad, because obviously she didn’t feel safe leaving just a letter; someone else could have found that.”

“Oh get back, I know,” said Ham, propping himself on an elbow. “These suckers are going to blast away this whole island, aren’t they?”

Tom slapped his forehead. Di coughed to cover a laugh.

“What else?” said Thea. She was on her stomach still staring out to sea, doing slow push-ups. “Let’s focus on what we need to find out. The things we’re looking for, the answers we don’t have yet.”

“The unknowns,” said Oki.

"'Zactly," said Ham. "What were they talking about in that room, Di? I didn't hear anything."

"Ugh, me neither," Di said. "I heard about exactly two words. 'Stimulation' was one, I think. The other one was 'flushdrive' or something. That was something they wanted badly, whatever it is."

"Flash drive," said Oki. "Flash drive. It's a little computer chip thing where you can store a bunch of files. I bet that's what they was lookin' for up in town, in the trailers. She must have left it for you to find, Mrs. Clarke. What other clues were there? Shoot, maybe you already got it, Di."

"I don't *know* what a flash drive is," Di said, "and I sure didn't take one from Mrs. Clarke's trailer. Don't you think I'd know? I was there! Tom?"

"Think," Oki said. "Just think hard, would you? It's about the size of a nail clipper, and has a little cap on it. Either you got it, or she must've told you where it is with one of those clues."

Di was upset. She felt like she was constantly being blamed, first by the security man, then by the Poets, and now by Oki and everyone else.

"We took straws, OK?" she said. "Stirring straws, that's it."

"Regular stirring straws?" Oki said. "Oh man, that ain't it. It don't fit in no straw. It would be in some container, ideally, to keep dry and safe." The group grew quiet. Embarrassed. Staring out at the water again. A hopeless sensation tugged at Di's thoughts, and it seemed contagious. Lost at sea.

"A saltshaker too," said a voice, softly. Tom. "We took a saltshaker out of there too, and I remember seeing something dark down in the salt. My dad's got it. It's in the Kebab Kart."

Some days it seems like you can't walk two steps without some clown telling you how to improve your thinking or your creativity or whatever. You're playing a video game or doing Jumble or Sudoku, and pretty soon someone is giving you a lecture about how that improves your brain. Like that's going to make you the next Einstein or an astronaut or a genius problem solver.

But that didn't seem 100 percent true, Di was thinking. Real problems, they're not set up like puzzles. You don't always know where to start. You're not sure there is a solution. You have not a freakin' clue you can find one if it exists.

You're a rat lost in a maze, pretty much. You sniff around and bump into walls. Maybe you make the right turn by accident, or maybe you see something, a little light, nothing more. Just enough to get you thinking about what to try next. Smarter people would probably see the solution sooner. Crotona kids maybe, those gifted-program Croutons with their tutors and their mom or dad who's already a doctor or scientist.

Yeah, Di thought: Maybe.

In the early morning hours of that Friday, with the tide low and the sea on a slow boil, Thea led the group along the lower edge of the island, in and out of small coves and over rock outcroppings where the water was too high. Here, out of the tunnels and off the island proper, it was as if they could see everything from grandstands. The island, the plant. The pattern of tunnels. The cliffs, and themselves too, crawling around the edges. That very first clue, the straws and saltshaker—the three, four, and five—had helped unlock everything. It had given them the triangle rule.

The triangle had given them the coordinates, (0, 0) and (12, 8), and then the slopes. Cartesian coordinates, Oki called them, named after a French guy from two million years back who showed that equations you wrote down on paper could describe stuff that happened in the real world. Kind of like the way that you could figure out where you were in the tunnels using the x- and y-pipes and the other clues.

That seemed kind of obvious now, and it wasn't really clear to Di why this Descartes (that was his name) got so famous just for that.

Then there was pi.

Pi had given them the circles into the plant and a way to estimate the distances. That included the distance they had to travel right now, from the positive x-axis to the negative y—the Point. That was exactly one quarter of the circumference of the total island, or $\frac{1}{4} \times (2 \times 3.14 \times 1{,}500) = 2{,}355$ yards, or long paces.

Di asked Oki about pi as they were climbing along. Was pi the only number like that, where you couldn't calculate it exactly?

"No," he answered. "No, no, no, no. There's infinity of them. That's called a real number, pi is one, and to me that's a good name for 'em because they are kind of more real for me than the other numbers."

"What do you mean, more real?" Di said.

Oki looked out at the water and continued. "Real numbers are in between the counting numbers, like one, two, three, and so on. And they're in between all the numbers you can write as fractions, like one-third or seven-nineteenths or whatnot."

"Is that possible?" Di said. "You can get pretty tiny with those fractions, like how about one over a billion or something."

"Yeah, it's possible—look at pi. And the square root of two is another one. If you got a right triangle with each short side one yard long, then the long side is the square root of two. That's a real number too."

"Really?" Di said. "Did Pythagoras know that?"

Oki laughed. "I hear he did, yeah. I don't think he liked it, though, is what I heard. Look out there, see those buoys?" He was pointing to a string of bobbing buoys, lighted, which marked a safe shipping lane past the island.

"Yeah, I see 'em," Di said.

"See, that's how I think about it. Those buoys are like the

counting numbers, what they call the integers: one, two, three, and all the way up. The fractions are kind of like the rope between each buoy. And the real numbers like pi are the water. The counting numbers are like markers along the way. That's all they are."

A few of their next moves were obvious, and they all knew it. Tom would snag the shaker from his dad, and pronto. Oki would connect it to a computer to see what was on it. Then at least they might have a better idea of what Mrs. Clarke was directing them to do at the plant.

In his quick circuit of the plant's console room, Tom had in fact found a computer. He had touched the keyboard and, sure enough, seen an electronic desktop with dozens of files. But he could do no more than that, he told them, because of course the machine wanted a login and a password to enter.

He remembered that the password had five digits. He was dead sure of that.

"Oh man, of course," Ham said. "How we gonna get through that, if that's what we need to do? One in a billion we figure that out."

"No it ain't," said Oki. "It's more like one in three hundred thousand, at most. And we can narrow it down. I'll show you how. I'll show you how you can break a code like that."

The Point was close now, and a trace of gunpowder light had softened the sky. A practical problem also loomed, as hard and real as the cliffs, one that could not be calculated with numbers or computers: Where would Di and Tom go?

Oki and Thea could easily disappear back into Adjacent; no one knew they were involved in this or expected them at school. Ham, as the island's most disturbed youth, could also come and go as he wanted. They'd have some explaining to do to their parents, but these were Adjacent kids; they knew how to tell stories.

Di and Tom didn't have such freedom. Mr. Pink had almost certainly seen her running away, and he knew that she and Tom were friends. They were suspects, and it was not safe for them to be seen—anywhere.

"We have to disappear, don't we?" Di said. She was turning her wrist. Tom nodded, looking up at the cliffs, lost in his own calculations. His mind was fluttering again, lifting up high, and he could see the perfect circle of the island, the x- and y-axes, triangle patterns in the broken quilt of trailers. And suddenly he saw the answer. It was an unusual sensation. He saw for the first time he could solve a problem involving reading other people, not numbers and patterns.

"Yeah, we do need to vanish," he said. "But I got an idea where."

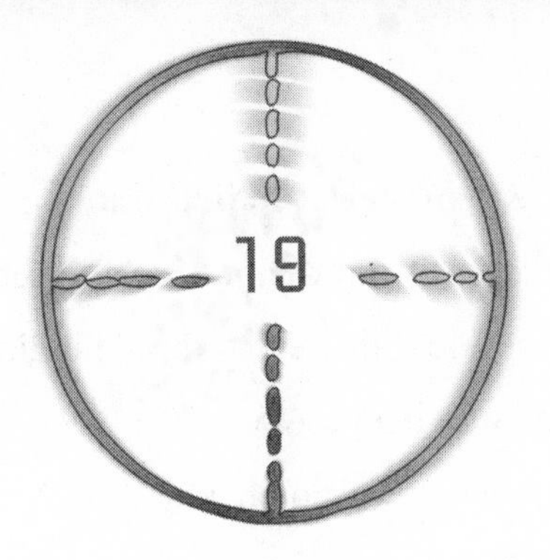

THE INVISIBLE ROOM

SECRET AGENTS HAVE THE LIFE. THEY REALLY DO. International spies, like not only do they travel all around Berlin, Germany, and whatnot, but also they have safe houses. Have you heard of that? Where you vanish, not by magic but for real. People take care of you there, with good food, sodas, and nobody outside knows where you are, and there's no homework or anything. You're just—gone.

The thing about disappearing, though, is that it's a lot harder to do if you're already invisible. Say, if you were born that way. Di was a local, Adjacent was all she knew, and it never occurred to her that someone would be looking for her other than her mom, or Noname the hound. The best idea she had was to hide out in the bus graveyard. But Tom Jones was what we called a tourist; he was born somewhere else, back in Iraq or Arabia or wherever. He was a master at hiding out, for sure, and yet he also watched Adjacent from the outside and sensed how people treated each other. He didn't even know he did that until now, when he figured out where to go.

"Well, lookit what we got here," said Mrs. Polya, as she opened her door for Di and Tom.

The pair of them had moved across Adjacent on the low road, as we called it: from crawl space to crawl space. At Tom's they had found the Kebab Kart, entered from below, through a floor panel, and found the saltshaker. Tom now clutched the flash drive in his sweaty fist.

Mrs. Polya motioned them in with a nod of her head.

Her trailer was attached to the store, behind the back-wall cooler, and Di noticed a few cases of beer on the trailer floor. The woman stuck her head out the door for a quick look around, locked it, then led her visitors to a corner of her tiny trailer. There she pushed through a small closet, and led them into a hidden room. A card table, a pair of cots, chairs: it was like she had been expecting them, Di thought.

Without a word their host served them bowls of stew, with slices of bread, cream sodas, and ice cream sandwiches. It all tasted so shockingly, stunningly, outrageously good that they lost all control. Everything was gone in minutes. A deep, rolling burp shook Tom's body, and he mumbled something resembling "sorry."

Mrs. Polya just chuckled. She was seated across from them now, in the tiny room, and in the dim light Di thought the older woman looked almost pretty: thin, sharp features, dark eyes, a girlish face, like some old-time ballerina.

"Listen to me," Mrs. Polya said. "First, I will let your parents know that you're OK, and do so discreetly. But you knew I could do that; that's why you're here. That and the dinner menu, anyway."

She stopped and smiled again, this time as if she had a secret. "The second thing is, I had another visitor. Last night. Maurice Kline. Do you know Maurice? Of course you do, you call him Big Sip. He was one of my son George's friends when they were back in high school. Maurice could never speak very well, but when George died, poor Maurice lost it entirely."

"Huh?" said Di. "Big Sip—what does he have to do with—"

"I don't know, dear," Mrs. Polya said. "Mrs. Clarke apparently told him something to pass on to you two, but even I can't understand Maurice so well. You know how he is. He seemed to say something about drawing circles in the dirt, I don't know."

"Oh!" said Di. "That's where I saw that tunnel map before—that's what Big Sip must've been tracing out all that time!"

"It doesn't surprise me," Mrs. Polya said. "Maurice actually worked for a while cleaning those tunnels when he was in high school. People forget, but they built those tunnels partly for us, for the workers who installed the machines, who maintained them and removed the toxic waste. They kept them up too, at least for a while. Maurice loved that job. He and George would—" She stopped, looked down at her hands, and kept looking at them for a while. Then she looked back across the table at Di and Tom. "Well, Maurice was trying to pass on something else to you two, something important. He has been trying to do that for a while, through me, and I have guessed for some time that you two and your friend Hamilton—I'm sorry, Ham—that you've been trying to put a stop to this awful searching and intimidation that the plant people are up to. They are trying to drive us away, off the island, that seems obvious."

Mrs. Polya gave them a level look. "Anyway, I wrote down everything from Maurice I could make out. The poor, sweet man ran away before I was absolutely sure what he was trying to say."

She handed them a torn envelope. On the back she had written:

Find the three digits in the amulet.
Find them in the Greek coin.

"A Greek symbol?!" Di said. "Ohhh, I hate this. Why does everything have to be some stupid puzzle?"

She began swiveling her wrist. She felt that she was on the

verge of learning something very important but was too slow or dense to get it.

"Amulet? What's that?" said Tom. He was leaning forward and had his hat tipped up, so you could see his face. What's happening to Tom? thought Di.

"It means different things to different people," Mrs. Polya said. "But here's what the dictionary says: 'A charm often inscribed with a magic incantation or symbol to protect the wearer from evil.'"

"Can you believe this?" Di looked disgusted now. "Magic incant-whatever. Next thing you know we're going to have some freakin' talking bear leading us into a magic castle. I swear."

Tom smiled widely and said, in a bear voice, "Come, follow me, children, to the forest!"

Di snorted. "Will we meet magic centaurs there, O noble king Mr. Bear?" and the two of them collapsed to the table, not laughing as bad as underground, but pretty bad.

Di finally caught herself and remembered that she and Tom were guests. "Um, Mrs. Polya, so, lemme see—so, thank you so much, from both of us, I mean so much, and if there's more ice cream sandwiches I know my mom will pay—"

"Oh honey," said Mrs. Polya, and right there she smiled in a sad way and put her head in her hands. Was she crying? Why?

Di looked over at Tom, who shrugged.

"No," Mrs. Polya said, finally. "Thank you, Lady Di. And

Tom. Both of you. We have needed you, Adjacent has, and I had no idea until now."

With that, the woman stood up, went back into her room, and came back with two more ice cream sandwiches.

"All right, you two, enough talking for now." Mrs. Polya was whispering. "You will stay right here, under cover, until dark."

THE AMULET

HERE'S ONE THING TO KNOW IF YOU EVER COME TO VISIT Adjacent. Wait—forget that. No one with half a brain has ever visited; no one with a quarter of a brain, or a single brain cell, has ever visited. But if you did, like on a field trip to see what a trailer park full of freaks next to a nuclear plant looks like, then you should take the late-afternoon ferry. Seriously, you don't want to be here when it's 120 degrees and dusty and there's a billion flies and plastic water bottles from Trashmore all over the place.

But when the sun starts to go down, a nice breeze picks up, and people kind of come out and mosey around Polya's store and the Broken Bamboo bar. Rene D. sometimes does card tricks out there, if he's not terrorizing somebody. And Pascal, with his big, deep voice, does some killer imitations of people. The bar too, before the serious drinking starts, it's pretty great. A few parents are in there, and Mr. Maoreli, the bartender, opens the doors wide and has music playing. Jazz and soul stuff, like from the big city.

None of that was happening now, because of all the security patrols and flares and checkpoints. Evening was dead. When Di and Tom, after sleeping through the day, ducked out of Mrs. Polya's, dusk fell like gold dust over an island so silent and spooky that it could have been inhabited by nothing but corpses and ghost snakes.

The cool, thick evening air ran through their bodies like some river of new life. Security vehicles were still patrolling the area but they could no more catch shadows than supercomputers could capture pi. Here finally was a chance to solve some clues with some help, Di thought. And a little time.

Bad news greeted them at Oki's place. The boy was there, and Hog, the old man, and Thea and Ham.

"They're patrolling around Trashmore," Thea said. She was looking through a pair of cheap binoculars. She handed them to Di. "Here, look." The binoculars seemed if anything to blur the image. Still, Di could see, and so could Tom, the lights and vehicles moving around Trashmore in the distance.

"They must know you get in that way," the old man rambled. "Think of it this way: They's all got to hang around that stinkhole cuz of you. With the rats and roaches and half-eaten sushi. Heh-heh!"

"Oh no," Di said. "Are we going to be able to go back down—"

"Don't worry about that for now. That's mine to figure out," Thea said. Di shrugged.

"OK, right," Di said. "C'mon in, then." The five of them shuffled around to form a circle, pulling tires up around Hog, who had his back to his trailer and looked ready to charge into the tunnels himself. Di studied the faces: Oki and Thea on her left, their eyes practically on fire; Tom with his hat brim up, intense; and Ham, who looked like he'd just planted a smoke bomb in someone's backpack. Like his old twisted self, essentially.

"Tom?" she said.

Tom nodded and held the flash drive up, between his index finger and thumb, in the light.

"Whoa," someone said, and several hands from the circle reached for the drive. Tom placed it in one, the thin grasp of Oki. Oki unfolded himself from his crouch, turned around toward the trailer, and inserted the drive into a small laptop he had on the trailer stoop. The others gathered around.

"Yup," he said. "This is an abort drive. A system bomb. Put this in a plant computer and launch the program on here, and it will bring their whole system to a dead stop." The boy turned to Hog. "Tell 'em, Pop."

Hog tipped back in his chair and cleared his throat. He

looked almost—well, happy, Di thought. "Folsom Energy, like all nuclear plants, is on a nationwide emergency grid," the old man said. "If their system fails, federal investigators will be down on them like white on rice. They'll take the place over."

"So?" said Di. "So what?"

"Stimulation, is what," Hog said. "Oki told me that was the word you heard. Well, almost. The word is 'simulation.' That's the word we used to have at the plant for a fake radiation leak. Like a fire drill at school. Those jokers want us all off the island. Everyone. If they stage that leak, they can get the place condemned off-limits for human habitation, and good-bye Adjacent, for good."

He paused. "Oki, you want to tell them the rest?"

Little Oki Koulu was in his crouch on a tire next to the old man, staring up at Hog like he was the President of the United States or something. "Yeah, I do," Oki said. "Pop says that they want the whole island for themselves, to get rid of nuclear waste. We's in the way. They means to fill those tunnels with toxic waste. But they can't do that with us livin' here. It's illegal, right, Pop?"

Hog snorted. "They're backed up. It costs a lot of money to ship all that waste to the desert down south, away from populated areas. They probably plan to use the tunnels to buy time, but they can't risk someone seeing 'em. It's a desperate plan, but it's not like they get a lot of help, either. Crotona and the towns on the mainland just want our electricity; don't care or even think about the waste. They're happy to make it someone else's problem, like they do with Trashmore. The point is, if you shut the plant's system down, there's no staged leak, the feds come in, and we get to keep living the good life, right here in paradise."

The others took a few moments to digest it all. The most baffling thing was that, after all the adventure, this was just a waste problem. Adjacent was the garbage capitol of the free world; it never occurred to any of them that garbage could be a bigger problem than it already was.

"Oh, man," said Ham. He was playing a pair of air conga drums. "Oh, that is absurdly raw, when you think about it. Right here in Adjacent, son! Oh, we gotta watch them try to jam all that nuke stuff into the tunnels. I'm not missing that for nothing."

Tom spoke up. "Ham! That's what we're supposed to stop from happening, don't you see?"

Ham stopped playing the air congas and pointed a finger at Tom. "You, professor man, gots a case of the 'zactlies. My bad. It would be raw to watch it, is all I was saying."

Di jumped up and put two fists in the air; she couldn't help herself. "Yes!" she said. "I mean no, we're not going to watch it, but yes we are so close to this, and we've got more to do, me and Tom do."

The FC thinking circle was breaking down. It was dark now, Oki had lighted a lantern, and it was like everyone just drank some maniac potion. Thea was in motion somewhere outside the light; Ham was on his back, moving his arms and legs like an overturned beetle. Tom and Oki were zinging pebbles at each other.

Di stood on her tire and said, "Stop! Just stop, OK? We got more to solve. Quick, bring the circle back in." No one listened. She waited, tried again. "Hey, look! I brought some cream sodas and BBQ sunflower seeds from Polya's. The spicy kind!"

That did it. Everyone was starving, and within minutes two whole bags of Polya's BBQ seeds were gone.

The thinking circle re-formed, Tom and Ham to Di's right, Thea and Oki seated to her left, and Hog directly across. He cried out, "Now stay put, you little rats, and listen to what the girl is saying. You still gotta figure out the password."

Di told them what Big Sip had grunted to Mrs. Polya about the amulet, or Greek coin. "He said, 'You can get the digits out of the Greek amulet.'" She recited the definition of amulet. She looked over at the others. Never in human history had four eager faces turned so blank so quickly, she thought.

Oki absentmindedly started fishing in his pockets, and the others imitated him without thinking, like it was contagious. In seconds they were all emptying the contents of their pockets and dumping stuff on the overturned oil drum at the center of the circle. A pair of nail clippers, a couple of black nickels, a broken comb, a few marbles, a small magnifying glass. Twine, a penknife, a folded-up baseball card, a half-eaten jawbreaker, three shiny rocks, a lizard skull. And of course cell phones. Every kid in Adjacent carried around a broken cell phone fished from Trashmore, at all times.

"Look," said Di. "Me and Tom—well, we've been following these clues from the beginning, you know, and it helps to think of things in different ways. Like maybe this amulet thing is not a coin. Like maybe it's something else."

More empty stares.

She turned to Tom. "You want to tell them what you can do with your mind, the way it transforms things and stuff?"

Mistake, she saw that immediately. He would never tell other kids about his visions. Ever. He was upset and snatched the baseball card, one of the stones, and the lizard skull from the drum. He rubbed the lizard skull, stood, and stepped out of the circle.

Then, miraculously, Tom spoke up, clear and angry. "Let's look at the map. Maybe there's some hint of where this thing is in there."

"How so?" Thea said.

"Because." He sounded like he was lecturing a group of dumb children now. "Everything was set up to give us the map. The triangle rule, OK? The slopes, the tunnels. The map, this map, everything we've done has been worked out on the map. Everything comes back to it."

He pulled out his copy and flattened it out on the drum. It was folded and musty and looked like this:

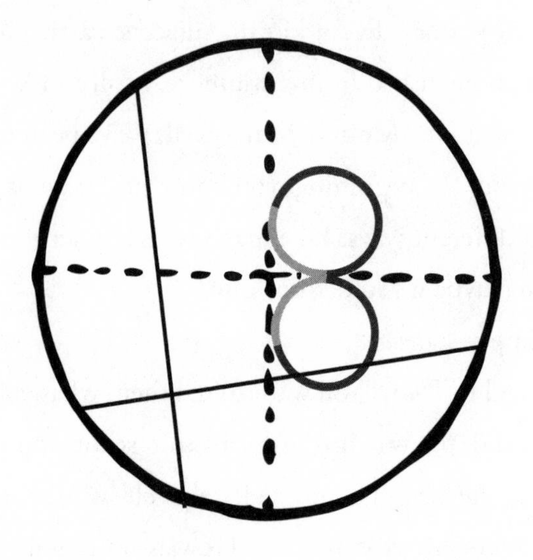

They looked at it for a long time. Tom turned it now and then so each person could see it from a different angle. They knelt there, as if in prayer, and Di had that sensation again, like the five of them, plus Hog, were sitting at the edge of the world trying to save civilization. She imagined six brains circling the map, getting stronger.

"What did Big Sip say again? Get three of the numbers out?" Ham said.

Di nodded. "Yep."

"I don't see anything," said Ham. "I mean, it's a map. It kinda looks like a face, if you ask me. Look, it's smiling a twisted smile at us. Whaddup, clown. Why you staring at me like that? Tell us the numbers, you freak."

"I see a number. If that means anything," said Oki. He pointed. "There," he said. The number four.

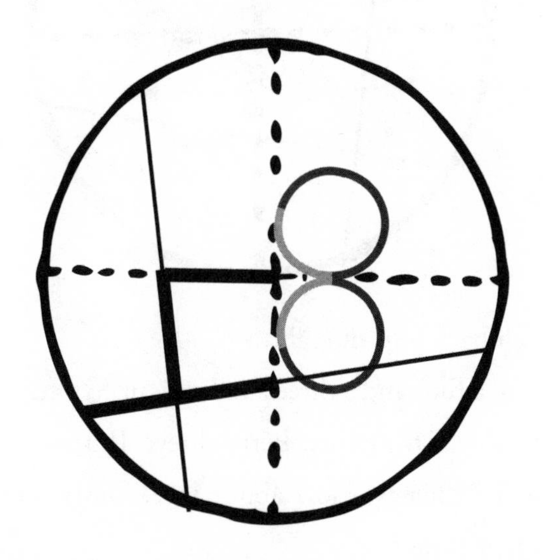

And there it was. Not a big deal. Maybe nothing, really. But it was a four.

"Four, like there are four pie pieces. Four quadrants on the map," Oki said. "Of course, that doesn't tell us where the amulet or coin is."

"Oooh!" It was Thea. "Oh. Do I put my hand up? It's been a long time since I been in a classroom. And this may be nothing. It's almost cheating, it's not even—"

"Bring it," said Di. "Uh, I mean, please."

"There," she said, pointing. "A three. Or maybe it's an eight."

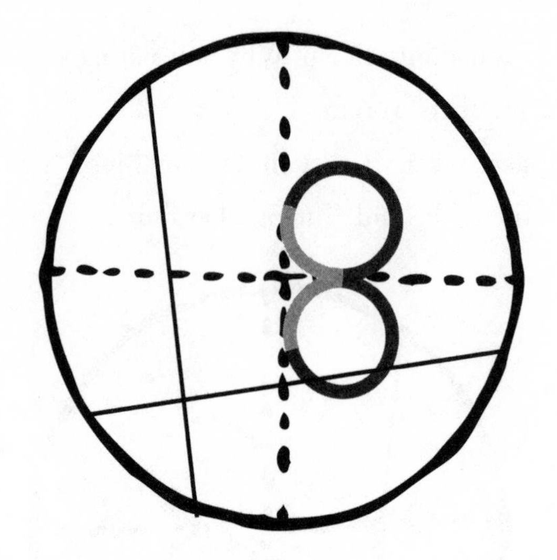

They fell back into thought.

They had a four and a three and an eight. Or maybe just one or two of those. Or neither. Forty-three? Thirty-eight? Maybe they were coordinates. How about three times four? Twelve. What did that mean?

"How many digits in that password, did you say?" said Ham.

"Five," said Tom.

Ham whistled. "Yeah, right. We're going to break that any minute now, by him seeing hallucinations in this clown map."

"OK," Di said. "Four, like there are four pie pieces. And three, like three circles. Not sure what to do with the eight."

"Three circles? There are only two," Ham said, pointing at the two circle tunnels.

"The island itself, OK?" said Di. "That's a circle, right? It's on the map, and that's what we're looking at. Look at the whole thing."

They stared again at it. Shifted and fidgeted, mumbling to themselves. When you're thinking, you're moving, and when you're moving, you're hunting. Maybe they had something and maybe they didn't. It certainly wasn't enough, one three and one four and one eight.

Di was starting to plot a strategy, with one person going to check (-4, 3) and another (-4, -8) and so on.

Tom stood up. "Hold on," he said. "Is the map complete?" No one knew what he was talking about. "It's not," he said. "We've just drawn all the tunnels we took, but there's more of them in there. Let's draw in everything. Every feature, every tunnel. Every man-made tunnel, anyway. And put the Point on there. All of it."

Ham sighed heavily. Di saw the maniac light glow dimly in his eyes. He would not sit still for long.

No one had even mentioned the tunnels yet, and she thought she knew why. With the Trashmore opening blocked, they would have to go down again, and going around the base of the island and scaling back up and in through the mouth of the x-pipe—she couldn't imagine actually doing all that again. She turned to Ham. "Ham, you're the one who knows those tunnels the best. You explored them first and stuff. You draw some in. Even if they're blocked, the ones you've seen."

She had no hope for this suggestion as anything more than a distraction for Ham. He took the pencil from Tom and completed the two straight tunnels they had taken to get to the negative half of the y-axis. He then added two others he knew about.

They stared again. "Check it out, you add one more line and you got a star. Cool," Ham said. Hamilton Rowan: He made a contribution.

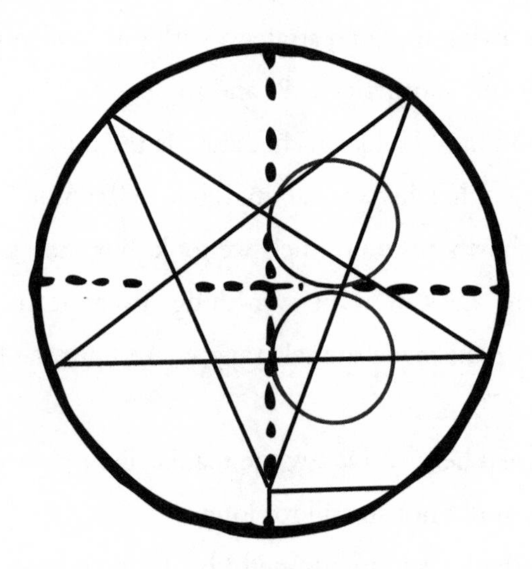

Di gasped to herself. This was it: the skull with the lopsided smile. The face in her dreams; not a face at all. All this time her brain had been working on the freaking map, even while asleep.

"Unreal," said Di. "You also got a five in there. See? Upside down."

"Yes, girl, you do," said Thea.

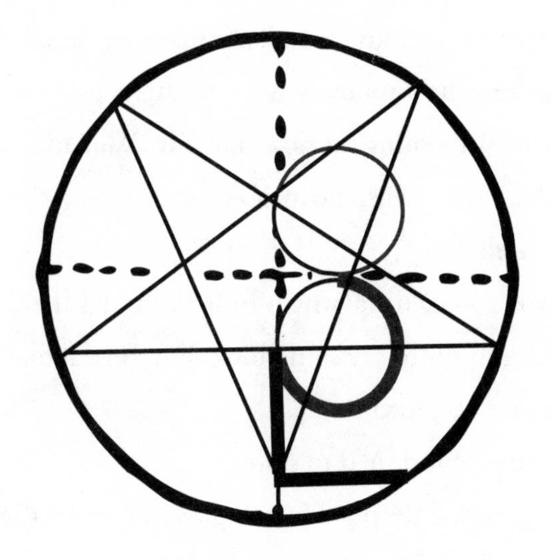

At this Tom stood up again and began pacing, staring at the sky. The surf was up now; he could hear breakers exploding against the cliffs, shaking the island. Tom's brain was turning on its side again too. He paced out into the darkness, knowing the others were waiting for him. He looked up at the stars and saw a great circle form, and silver tracers, forming the map's interior lines. He had been so wrong about so much, Tom saw. He had always assumed that his strange visions were like a hole in his brain, a deformity. Yet it was through that hole that he now saw the solution. He'd never really risked screwing up by throwing his ideas out in front of others, and here he was, about to do just that—embarrassment was itself a part of problem-solving, the public reflection of an active mind. Most of all, he'd always assumed that shapes and numbers and patterns were what made his mind get up and go on walkabout. Now he saw that it was the opposite: The problems were what helped his brain stay home, with something to do. Like Mr. Williams, their math teacher, had said, with no problems to solve, the brain will gorge on itself.

Everyone looked up when Tom reentered the circle. Ham opened his mouth to say something, but Tom spoke first.

"We have it," he said.

The others continued to stare.

Tom breathed deeply. He was physically widening his eyes, staring into their faces, Di noticed. He took his hat off. "The same numbers. Well, we have them—three, four, and five. The eight doesn't belong. The clue said three numbers. Three, four, five. Those have been the numbers all along. Three, four, five in the straws. Radius three, slopes four and one-fifth—one over five. Three, four, five. Those are the numbers."

"Then where's the amulet?" said Oki.

"Don't you see what he's saying?" Di said. "The map is the amulet. It is the charm. The map *is* the symbol."

"Oh, oh man, won't you lookit that," Oki said. "I shoulda seen it. That's the Pythagorean symbol! That five-point star in the circle. It's not exact, but it's pretty close. That was the symbol of the secret club. Pythagoras's club."

"I thought it was the symbol of the devil, or something." Typical Ham. He would know that, Di thought.

"No," Oki said. "I mean, maybe that's right, in some book or something. You'd have to ask Pop, he knows all this stuff. But this was the Pythagorean symbol first." The old man Hog smiled. It took several beats for all of this to sink in.

Then Thea, looking her old sullen self, threw cold water on it. "Yeah, but the password is five digits. Five. There must be thousands of ways you can put three, four, and five into that, if you use other numbers," she said.

"No, no, no," said Oki. He was smiling broadly now. "Less than that, much less than that—if you keep the three-four-five in order."

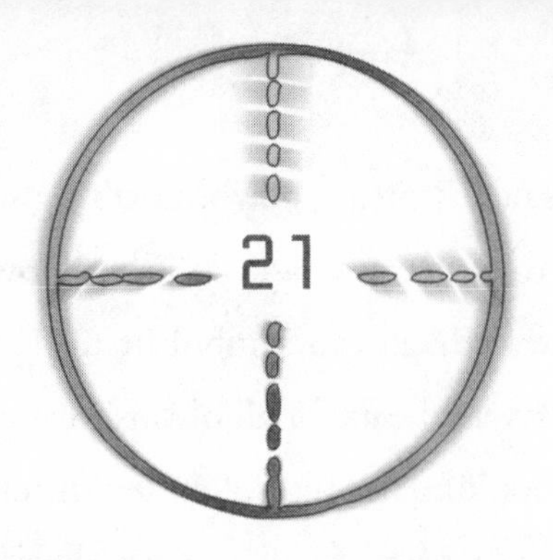

BRUTE FORCE

ONE THING YOU CAN SAY FOR MATH TESTS, AS HEINOUS as those suckers are, is at least when you've done all your sweating, you can stand up and leave. All right, there's always some clown or two or three in the class who's handed the thing in early, and they're sitting there tapping their pencil or reading, all relaxed and stuff like they could do it in their sleep. That's what spitballs were invented for, if you study their history.

The point is, though, that after solving those kinds of problems you don't have to go out and do anything. Amen to that—doing nothing. In Adjacent we had a lot of practice doing that, and role models too. Half of the entire population of the island were world experts in doing nothing, and planned their day around it. Sleep in, sit on your stoop in your underwear, yell stuff at people, maybe try to find your flip-flops later in the day to head over to the Bamboo. Mr. Devlin has said out loud a couple of times that he could do less in one day than any challenger. Ham's dad, Mr. Rowan, could probably take him one-on-one, is what people say, but Mr. Rowan's too lazy for any competition that doesn't include cards and whiskey.

Di, Tom, and the others needed to act, and they knew it. After a dinner of beans and potatoes prepared by Hog, they all took a break and scattered, thinking about what was ahead. Oki said he would figure out a way for them to determine the password quickly given the numbers they had, and that at least gave them the sense that they would soon have all they needed for the mission.

Di and Tom were relieved at first that someone else who was good at math was helping with the clues. But they felt they owned these problems, they wanted to solve it themselves, and started thinking about how many ways three, four, and five could go into a five-digit password.

"It would depend on whether the numbers went in that order," Di said. The two of them were off by themselves, sitting on the hood of a rusted-out VW near the cliffs. "It would also depend on whether letters were allowed in the password. If so, there's a whole lot more possible answers."

"Yep," Tom said. "But if the three-four-five is in order, you can think of that as one number, can't you? I mean, if there are only five digits, then the three-four-five can only be in one of three places. At the beginning. In the middle. Or at the end."

Those possibilities had lined up in their heads: (3, 4, 5, _, _); or (_, 3, 4, 5, _); or (_, _, 3, 4, 5). The blank spaces could be any number from 0 to 9.

"Of course, that doesn't mean the three, four, and five are together," Tom said.

When they rejoined the group, everyone had moved inside Oki's trailer. Di looked around in awe. Stacks of computer equipment, some of it very old, crowded every corner. A hard drive sat upside down in the sink. Cords crisscrossed the floor. Oki and Thea were seated on overturned crates in front of a live screen, their faces swimming in blue light.

Di resisted the urge to ask where exactly everyone slept, or where the fridge was. How did Hog cook? Where did they eat? She thought of how little she knew about how people in Far Corner lived. Or about how anyone lived, for that matter.

Oki turned from the screen to face the others.

"OK, we're going to break a password. And you'll see, we don't need any tricks or supercomputers to do it," he said.

He explained the strategy slowly. The first step was exactly as Di and Tom had reasoned: Assume that the 3-4-5 came as a package, in that order. If so, that trio could be in only one of three places.

If it was at the beginning, that left two open spaces at the end. Each of those two spaces could have any number from 0 to 9 in it.

"For each number in that fourth space," Oki said, "you can have ten choices in the fifth space. Do you see that?" He turned and pointed an open hand at the screen. "Look." The screen listed all the possibilities, if the fourth space was a zero:

(3, 4, 5) 0, 0

(3, 4, 5) 0, 1

(3, 4, 5) 0, 2

. . . and so on.

"This little sucker just rips, seriously," said Ham, who was straddling two upside-down computers. He turned to Hog, who was wedged between a stack of electronic stuff and the wall. "Did you teach him all this, Hog-man?"

Hog kicked Ham in the shin. "Just listen up, sonny Jim. Mathematics isn't some secret language. It's for everybody. It's for the millions. If you stood on your hind legs and paid attention for two seconds, you'd see that. And no, Oki don't need my help."

"So," Oki said, "ten possible choices for the fourth space, and ten for the fifth. And ten times ten equals one hundred—one hundred possible passwords, altogether. Easy."

"If the three-four-five is at the front," said Ham.

"Right. Of course," said Oki. "But you can see that you

also have a hundred choices when the three-four-five is in the middle, and another hundred when it's at the end. See? In all three cases you got two open spaces, which could have any of number between zero and nine."

That is, the password could be any of 100 + 100 + 100 = 300 sequences.

"It seems like a lot," Oki said. "It ain't. We got five people here, so three hundred divided by five is sixty. Each person gets sixty of 'em and we plug those in."

He reached down and picked up an old box and put it on his lap. He rifled around in it and began pulling out what looked like old calculator keypads—which they were—and handed out one to each person.

"I can wire these to a filter, which connects to the computer and feeds it the passwords one at a time," he said. He held up some index cards. "I made a list of sixty for everybody. All you gotta do is punch in those numbers fast—and accurately—and we will cover every possibility."

He looked over at Hog and back at the others. "We timed it. You can punch in sixty in under two minutes, without even rushing that much. We should be able to crack the code quickly. That is—if we ever get back to that computer."

That was a big "if," and no one needed reminding. The password problem, as confusing as it was, had at least taken their minds off the tunnels. Now the thought of going back underground made them all quiet. Di was staring at her shoes; so was everyone else.

Tom broke the spell. "So, um, this is good. But what if letters are allowed too? Like what if the password can be three-four-five-A-B, or something?"

Oki looked up at Tom for a moment.

"Yeah," he said. "I thought about that. It's possible, of course. I made some lists of those too. But it's more than thirty-five hundred choices. I'm hoping we don't have to. I don't think we'll have that much time."

They were silent again, each trying not to imagine in too much detail what it might be like to be caught. Di concentrated on the password problem, with letters. She saw that, with 26 letters and 10 digits to choose from, there were 36 possible choices for each open space. So, 36 × 36 choices for each of the three possible locations of the 3-4-5 group. She put it in her calculator: 3 × 36 × 36 = 3,888 possible choices. She looked over at Tom and mouthed "thirty-six" and he nodded back.

Ham then opened his mouth to speak but Thea cut him off, answering his question before he could ask it.

"I said I would take care of getting us in there, OK?"

"Yeah, but how?" said Ham.

"You'll see."

No one wanted to hear about that, though, not in any detail. Not now. Di wondered if everyone else was even half as afraid as she was. A silence once more fell over the trailer, this time for a long while. It was well past midnight. They had the flash drive. They had their lists and keypads. They had a way in. The only thing left was to do it.

"What you dwarfs waiting for?" It was the old man. "You better get outta here soon. Like, around, I don't know—now? You got a lot to do." He reached over and gave Oki a small radio of some kind, wrapped in plastic. "You can call me on that, just in case you get—well, just in case."

OVER THE EDGE

SEE? SEE WHAT HAPPENS WHEN YOU PRAY FOR something dead twisted to go down, and it does? You're stuck having to do stuff you really don't want to do. Like, at all. The truth is that deep down all you really, really want to do is one thing: bail. Crack a cold soda in front of the TV, and call in a team of ninja warriors to finish the job. But you can't, because that's weak, and because there's no way out anyway. Our most trusted, most foolproof, and most elegant Adjacent solution—giving up—wasn't possible this time. Have you heard about those maniacs who first explored the river down in the Grand Canyon? In, like, Arizona or somewhere? A bunch of those guys bailed halfway through, because it got too hectic for them. They tried to hike out of the canyon and died. The guys who kept on riding the wild river, they made it out. And the main leader guy had one arm too. You can look this up on the Internet.

So the group headed out. Thea led them around the island, outside the perimeter of Adjacent. In the dark Di could make out the back of Mr. Devlin's trailer, and off by itself, Blue Moon's. The wind howled from behind, and a wave exploded below as they passed the Point. Like a row of ants they proceeded east, toward the plus side of the x-pipe. The giant plant security fence loomed off to their left, to the right the cliffs, and in between nothing but scrub, gravel, old tires, swirling garbage. Almost zero cover.

A searchlight from one of the plant's towers swept the area periodically, like some alien eyeball, making dust glow in the air. Di looked over her shoulder as they moved, and dodged the light when it came. It would be beyond pathetic to be caught here, in this nowhere empty lot.

The plant's fence-line ran close to the edge as they approached the eastern side of the island, nearing the spot above the mouth of the x-pipe. Thea stopped suddenly, spun, and looked up at the sky. "What the"—Di turned and looked—another searchlight, but from what?

The five hit the ground and scattered, looking for any cover at all. Passing high overhead, with a lazy thumping sound, was a helicopter, as huge as a spaceship it looked, dangling a light over the island. The light zigzagged right through where they were lying; impossible to say if it saw anything.

"What is going on? They can't be looking for us. A helicopter? Did you see how big it was? I've never seen one of those, except on TV. Omigod, did you see that?" Di couldn't stop talking or twirling her wrist.

"Oh, that was raw," Ham said. "I bet they got machine guns. Seriously. That looked like a Black Hawk copter. I'm kind of a scholar when it comes to that kind of stuff."

"OK, Professor, that's great. Whatever. We got to keep moving," Thea said. At the foot of the fence, where it nearly touched the edge of the island, Thea had tied a rope around a fence post. At the other end she had fashioned a kind of double loop. Di, Tom, and Oki all turned and looked back toward Adjacent, sensing what was coming.

"I'll go first," Ham said.

"I know you will," Thea said. "You go first, and you make sure that everyone gets into that rock shelf, and safely." She gave him a look.

He shrugged, grabbed the rope, put his feet into the loop, moved the rope up his legs to use as a harness—and slid feet-first over the edge. Just like that. Gone.

Thea had looped the rope around another post as well, Di saw, and used this as a leverage to lower Ham. She was all muscle, thought Di.

After a few minutes the rope slackened, and there was sharp tug. The lunatic had landed. Di, feeling faint, moved toward the edge a few steps as Thea pulled the rope back up.

"OK, Princess, you're up," Thea said. Holding the slack in a coil, Thea had Di step into the loops, one leg at time, and made the harness. Di could do nothing more than watch all this, numbly, as if it were happening to someone else. She heard a voice, coming from what seemed a long way away.

"Don't worry about climbing, OK?" Thea said. "Just hold on and look for Ham. You should recognize the shelf. It's about two thirds of the way down. OK? Say OK for me, will you? Once. All right, then nod your head. Can you at least do that?"

She must have succeeded. She looked over toward the edge and could not move, not even her wrist. Now hands were helping her walk and she could feel them shaking. Or was that her shaking? Helpless, compliant, being led off a cliff, like all of Adjacent, she thought. Another voice, gentle. "Like climbing down to the couch. Like going to the couch. The couch. And the couch is higher." Tom's.

At the edge she looked around wildly, grabbed desperately for Tom. And then there was nothing under her feet—and she was dangling in outer space. Swinging, spinning—why couldn't it stop?—eyes open but everything dark, blasting wind, spraying dust and debris like buckshot into her face, and the watery sound below. Yawning and roaring, heaving up and collapsing down, explosions, cutting the air with a razor salt sting. She thought suddenly of scrawled verse she'd seen on Virgil's notebook:

Through caverns measureless to man
Down to a sunless sea

She felt her grip weaken and put her whole mind to holding, holding. Holdtherope. Black shapes now—birds?—moving in and out of the cliff. Eyes too, animal eyes, peering out of cracks in the wall. Laughing at her. Her legs were running in the air, disgusting, stupid, like she was riding an invisible bicycle—she couldn't stop them—and then something wrapped around her right ankle, something strong and alive.

She screamed with all her might, let go of the rope, and dropped on her side in the air and almost out of the harness. She stopped breathing for a second.

Now something had grabbed her wrist and she stared wildly at it in the face—"Ham!" she yelled—and a few moments later it was over. She collapsed on the rock shelf, out of the wind, and lay there shaking and crying. Her eyes were pinned open; she couldn't close them.

"It's OK. It's OK. You did it. It's done. It's OK. That was the rawest thing I seen any eleven-year-old do, especially a girl. Beyond raw. Delta level. Seriously."

She barely recognized the voice. Ham's, unlike she'd heard it before. The shaking gradually eased to a tremble. She still couldn't get her eyes to close but she felt herself regaining control.

"A crazy ride, is what that was, and you did it," Ham was saying. He was focused on the next climber now, Oki, terrified, coughing and moaning as he was pulled in. Tom next, shaking badly, and soaked. The two of them lay there as if they'd just been saved from drowning. Which they pretty much had, Di thought.

Thea arrived a few moments later, climbing down the rope with no harness. Di wondered how anyone could grow up to be so fearless, ever. They reversed their climbing escape from the week before and found the mouth of the x-axis pipe as they had left it: cracked, open to the sea, deserted.

"Um, OK, everyone still has their keypads?" Di said, once the group was safely inside the pipe. She looked at Oki. "And the flash drive?"

Di could tell that Thea was annoyed. Thea liked being in charge, she thought. No reason to worry about that now; there were too many other things to worry about. Besides, Di thought, none of them would be here or have had a chance to fight back against the plant without herself and Tom. It was still their operation.

"We will follow Tom through the tunnels and into the plant. Then he and Ham can maybe scout from there. It's well after midnight, so there'll probably be people working in that basement part. I know my mom has to go in real early sometimes."

That last thought had just popped into her head. It was true: There was an early shift, and risk of getting spotted would be much higher than last time, which was before midnight. She had a private fear that the circle tunnel into the plant would be blocked, as Trashmore had been. It wasn't. They moved into the circular tunnel to the plant, and into the familiar seeping darkness, darkness beyond all light.

Di had felt at times in these tunnels that she was burrowing into the problem, even tunneling into the core of the math itself. This is what math felt like to her: hard, cold, dark, demanding. And when she emerged into the open air she felt like it was not a big deal, in the same way that problems, once solved, seemed smaller, not so hard.

Now she had another sensation, of slipping through the deepest wormholes in her own brain. What would it look like in there? Like this, she thought. Dark and damp and sticky. She imagined the anxious part of her brain to her right, grainy and bulging; and to her left the problem-solving area, smoother, warmer. A brain within a brain.

Down and down, into thought itself, to the very center, alone in the dark. She was so absorbed that she nearly ran over Oki, who had stopped in front of her. The plywood entrance, just ahead.

They were back.

THREEFOURFIVE

"MORE LIGHT THIS TIME," THEA MUMBLED. AND THERE WAS.

The plan, so far, seemed on track. None of them believed for a second that it would succeed—they were Adjacent kids—but they had not been caught and they drew more confidence from that than they knew.

"Keep it open," Di said, once they had slipped past the plywood door. "Just in case, on the way out." The early shift had begun, as Di had said. Peering from behind the processor, she could tell that it would not be as easy to get back to the computer terminal in the office upstairs. A constellation of lights glowed now in the great basement vault; the only cover was along the walls, where shadows pooled amid pipes and the rock wall.

A plant worker suddenly came into view, a sole figure in a yellow jumpsuit. There had to be others. The place felt alive, even over and above the din of the machines. A place where people were working.

"One thing at a time," she said. "Ham and Tom. Go and check the control room place. Just check it and come back."

Di noticed that her voice had settled down. It was no longer shaking, like out on the rock shelf. She was anxious, as usual, working her wrist, and at the same time thinking clearly. She was doing both. That repelling down the cliff must have burned out half of her fear nerves, she figured.

As long as she wasn't hanging off the edge of the planet, spinning like a spider in the wind, she was calm by comparison. Tom and Ham slipped over to the near wall and vanished into the shadows, and reappeared several minutes later, just below the metal staircase.

Here we go, Di thought.

The pair moved up the stairs easily. Di noticed that Tom had his cap off: a good sign. A glimpse of the red cap could get them busted instantly.

A loud crack suddenly rang out above the churning of the machines—and the door to the control room swung open. Tom and Ham, one landing below, quickly climbed into the dark space between the stair railing and the rock wall—but they were still visible, even from where Di and the others stood.

No one breathed as a trio of yellow-suited workers banged down the stairs, right by the intruders.

Di's heart was beating heavily in her head. She put her hands on her temples to try to control it, which helped some. She looked up to see Tom and Ham crouching by the door—and peering in. She made herself watch. The fluorescent glow coming through the window cast a spooky glow on half of Tom's face.

Thea and Oki, beside her, were dead silent.

First Tom, then Ham drew back from the door, checked below for yellow jumpsuits, and came back down the stairs, half-jogging. The three others watched, expecting a siren and flashing lights to explode any moment. None came. The two boys were back into the shadows now, and in minutes were back with the others, out of breath. Just seeing them back, Di felt a momentary wave of relief, a warm and dizzy sensation.

"No way," Ham said. "No way it happens in there. There are fifty people working in there. You couldn't get in there if you were invisible."

Di looked at Tom for confirmation.

He shook his head. "Packed."

That one word seemed to puncture the whole plan. A few seconds before, everything looked possible, doable. Now it seemed impossible.

"You know what?" Ham said. He was getting angry. "Let's pitch these kiddie toys"—he held up his keypad—"and climb down there where those generator things are and just throw a knife into them suckers. I'll do it. I don't care anymore. I hate this place. I hate it. What, we're up there living in freakin' shacks and they won't let us do even that?" He was losing his head. "My old man, yeah he's a drunk, but he's gonna get killed. Seriously, he's gonna get his gun when they try to evacuate him and they'll shoot him down. They'll shoot him down."

His face looked cold and sinister in the dim yellow light. "I mean, what is this nonsense about staging an accident?" Ham said. "Let's hurt these clowns."

"I agree," said Di. "Absolutely agree. Let's hurt 'em. One thing, though, long as we're down here." She stopped for a second and held up her hand. "Think for a second. This is a problem too. And it has a solution. We've been solving problems for months, that's how we got this far. Why should we stop now? Think. When you're thinking, you're moving"—she saw Tom roll his eyes at this but continued—like those workers, don't they take a break? I know my mom talks about that."

Thea was nodding her head. Even Ham was thinking about it. But when was break, exactly? Waiting around was a very risky strategy.

"Something else, then," she said. "C'mon."

Thea cleared her throat. "The uniforms," she said. "I'm big enough. Ham too. Go up there and pass in one of those, especially if there's a lot of people up there."

"You mean knock someone out and take one?" Oki said.

"Yes," said Ham. "That's what she means—yes."

Not likely, Di thought. She couldn't imagine anyone but Ham actually doing it, and he would mess it up somehow.

Besides, all five of them were needed to break the password in good time. And what if they were recognized up there? She could tell that the others weren't sold on the idea, either. "More ideas," Di said. "One or two. Turn it over in your heads. See it from above and below."

"How about looking for another tunnel?" Tom said. "Go back through here and look for another entrance. There has to be one." Dead on arrival, Di thought. That one retreat, back up the coastal path by the Point, was plenty. The tunnels were too unpredictable, and she could see that none of the others liked this idea.

Di noticed Oki nodding his head in a kind of trance.

"What?" she said.

"It's gotta be here," he said. "Look at the size of this place. Zero Level. You're telling me there's no computers down here? Zero? There's gotta be one, because the workers down here are going to need to check the plant systems too. Don't you think? There's got to be a terminal down here, we just ain't found it. We ain't really looked past that stairway."

Di could tell by Ham's body language that he was considering this. She nodded her head, to encourage him further.

She immediately thought of something Mrs. Clarke used to say, which always sounded stupid at the time: A mathematician running to escape a fire in a theater sees a bucket of water by the door. He picks up the bucket and douses the flames. It happens again, only now there's no bucket of water. What does he do? He puts a bucket of water by the door, and repeats the solution.

"If what you need isn't there, just put it there and see what happens," Mrs. Clarke would say. "Start with the solution and work backwards."

"OK," Di said. "Everyone who's with Oki put a hand up."

They all did, Ham reluctantly. Di decided that they should stay together this time. Being spread out and lost to one another in a room this big and this loud would be too risky; they had to work as a group if there was any chance of cracking the password.

Between the tunnel opening and the staircase there was very little to see. A couple of empty workbenches. A worker with a clipboard checking dials near the bottom of one of the block machines. A metal toolbox, leaking oil. Di estimated that they could see only about a quarter of the whole space, maybe less, because of the machines and other obstructions.

"Let's get past the stairs quick and see what's on the other side of the room," she whispered. "We've never really seen what's over there." Single file, they slipped through the narrow space between the staircase and the wall, as quickly as they could without running.

The far end of the room, which had been mostly invisible to them during the first visit, looked very much the same as the other parts, but Di could tell that the area was much larger than she had thought. The rows of processors still made it difficult to see much. Ham motioned for them to follow him out from the wall and behind one of the block machines. No turning back now, Di thought.

At least they had some cover. From machine to machine they crept, peering from behind each and seeing nothing. Something was happening up ahead, though. Di could feel the vibration of footsteps on the floor grating, and not only their own.

Ham peeked around still another of the processor machines, and drew back with a smile. "Magic," he said.

The others took a look, two at a time, and saw for themselves: computer terminals, maybe a half dozen, in a row of workstations, each staffed by a plant employee. From behind the machine the whole length of the row was visible, with the nearest plant worker no more than twenty feet away.

Di suddenly heard herself whisper, "Just do this." Up until now she had not believed they would get close, not really. She kneeled down, took deep breaths, and rubbed her temples again. Move on, she thought to herself. Think and move.

"There must be some with no workers, farther on," she said aloud.

As they crouched to advance farther, a bright green light flared somewhere above them and a piercing whistle sounded. Ham dropped immediately into a karate stance, Thea and Tom hit the floor, and Di and Oki put their hands up, as if they were being arrested. The game was up—this was the alarm, had to be—and Di for one was weak with fear. Relief too, that it was over.

But it wasn't. In the rolling din of this machine room it took them a few humiliating moments to realize that they had not been caught. No one was around. This was not an alarm. It was a minute before they understood what it was: a signal for a shift break. Peering around the edge of the processor, Di could see workers moving, headed maybe for a coffee table in back.

All except one, that is. An older man with safety glasses remained working at the terminals, blocking what would have been easy access to a computer. He stayed and stayed. The others looked too. Why didn't he take a break? What was he doing? Didn't he want a break? The corkscrew in Di's stomach was turning again.

She saw too that Ham was thinking about pouncing on the man. That would be a disaster. She had to think fast. It was Thea who put a hand on Ham's shoulder before he did anything. And it was Tom who, without saying a thing, slithered from behind the machine, slow as a python, and along the row of desks directly behind the man. He coiled under one desk and waited.

What was he doing? Tom . . . of all people, Di thought.

Again in slow motion Tom slid past the man's turned back and under the next desk, and the next. When he got to the end of the row, he reached up and grabbed something off a desk. He stayed under that desk for a while, watching the man, before moving slowly back. It took forever. One desk at a time. In the dim light Di realized it was very hard to see Tom—and she knew where he was. The escape artist. The invisible human. He had told her once that if you are visible—but not yet seen—you had to move slow. People noticed quick movements out of the corners of their eyes, he had said. Still, the work break had to end soon. Not much time left.

Tom finally slid back behind the machine and pulled something from under his shirt. It took Di a couple of beats to see that it was a computer. A laptop! Light, and small, but it was the real thing.

"You raw little righteous twisted freak," Ham said. "You scored, you Delta man."

Oki snatched the laptop from Tom, too eager. Di saw that the dark, small boy was sweating and praying to himself. He flipped the computer open and mouthed "wireless, wireless"—then made a fist, and crossed himself. "Yes," he said.

The others huddled around the screen and saw the prompt for username and password. It was happening.

Oki typed "Malba Clarke" into the username box, and then attached his sequencer. They all had their keypads out, and the boy swiftly wired each into his gadget. He crossed himself again, and nodded.

"Go," he said.

At that moment the green light flared again—break was over—and they froze for a second. Someone would soon be missing a laptop and start looking for it. Oki started typing madly and the others joined in. Kneeling and tapping, like a group of street kids with a stolen video game, and each time they glanced at the screen they saw the password space fill—and reject. Fill again—and reject.

Oki finished first and looked up with eager eyes at the screen. Nothing doing. Di felt his rising anxiety as a tightening in her own shoulders. She touched his arm and motioned with her head for him to have a look at the plant work group. Someone must be missing a laptop by now.

The boy took one peek around the edge of the block, pivoted fast, scooped the laptop with his palm—"move, around the next block," he said—and the others followed, trying to keep their individual wires slack. Desperate now. Shuffling together like a miniature chain gang back toward the staircase. They passed the next big processor, turned the corner, and held their breath.

"Keep working," Di mouthed. The screen was spitting back, "Login incorrect. Login incorrect."

Oki took another peek around the corner they had just turned. He still held the laptop in his palm and this time his widened eyes were enough to set the group in motion again.

Tom slid to the front and they followed by instinct without thinking, now into open space. How long could they make it out here? Di thought. She felt footsteps marching behind them somewhere and yet somehow no one was yelling.

Tom led them back toward the terminals, which seemed insane—"go, go, go," she heard herself saying—and then they were under a work bench, dark, with only the metal back of the desk standing between them and the workers on the other side.

"Hey!" someone yelled. "What was that? Over there!"

It had to happen, Di thought.

A few minutes and they were cooked. Ham finished, then Thea, Tom, and finally Di: "login incorrect," all the way around.

"Some clown screwed up," Ham said, turning to Tom. "Was it you, Jones?"

Oki shook his head. "No, no, no, no. The probability that one bad entry was the actual password is the same as if we just guessed wildly—very, very unlikely. There must be letters in the password."

Tom had slipped away again, Di noticed. Where? A pair of

legs came by the workbench, then another. A flashlight beam swept the floor very close.

"Here?" a woman's voice yelled.

She could barely be heard. The dim lights, and especially the waterfall hum of the machines, were now working for the intruders.

"We have to start guessing," Oki said. He looked at Di. "Educated guesses. A sequence she would have used. You're the one who knew her best. It's up to you now."

It was up to her now. She tipped her head back and waited for an idea. Total blank. Paralysis. Seasickness. Unbelievable.

After all this work she was digging deep and there was nothing there at all, nothing but her own familiar, annoying anxiety.

After everything! Crawling through all those tunnels, with spiders and rodents. Holding her breath and going through the puddle. Hanging off the edge of the planet. How close to dying she was then. How she could almost feel herself hitting the rocks below. Kicking her legs like an overturned beetle. Half her fear nerves burned out!

"It's stupid, but OK," she said, and entered Mrs. Clarke's initials with the 3-4-5. She had to at least do something.

"MC345."

No.

She tried "345MC."

No.

She tried "M345C."

The screen seemed to turn off. Total blank. Then a purplish glow, and a desktop with FOLSOM over the top.

"Welcome, Malba Tahan Clarke," the screen said.

Di had no idea how long all this took; it might have taken a half hour or three seconds. Oki grabbed the machine, inserted the flash drive, and immediately opened the file named pyth.345.

A prompt came: "Run pyth.345?"

Di saw him hit the return button and instantly felt two giant hands on her shoulders.

"What we got here, a rodent problem?" A screeching voice, familiar: Security Man, Mr. Brown. The one who had moved into Mrs. Clarke's trailer last summer. He and two others, in black jumpsuits with SECURITY in yellow on the back, had Oki and Ham, holding them by their collars, like you would a cat. Thea and Tom had gotten away.

"Deitz," said Security Man. "Track down the other two. Any means necessary, and I mean any. You understand? We have a Folsom team from headquarters hitting the island to lock us down. Nobody leaves. This is not a game. This is national security now."

Di was in a state beyond exhaustion and fear. You're going

to *need* "any means" to get Tom and Thea, she thought.

She looked at the others and noticed how tiny they were, Ham and Oki, next to the security men. The three of them formed a triangle, Di thought, and for a fraction of a second their eyes met in the center. Exactly the center? Di wondered. What was the exact center of a triangle? How would you figure that out, for any triangle?

She was losing her mind.

She had also noticed something in just those few moments, a look she saw in the faces of her two friends. Before being caught they had all expected to fail. Now caught, they all had a secret hope of success, she was sure of it. Oki had dropped the system bomb, hadn't he? She'd seen it with her own eyes: He hit return. Something had to happen.

"Mays, you follow me," Security Man was saying. "Let's throw these urchins into holding. One more thing—" And then something happened.

It was Tom Jones. He was standing on one of the humming boxes, waving his hat, looking large and shadowy beneath a beam of light. "*I got what you want, suckers!*" he shouted, holding up the flash drive. "*Come and get it if you can!*"

The security guards pivoted and stared at Tom, confused. Di gawked openly at the sight of him. Ham kicked free and jumped up on a desk, put a fist in the air, and started yelling,

"Tom Jones! Tom Jones! Tom Jones! Tom Jones!" He was out of control.

Oki dropped to the floor, pulled Di down with him, and they were loose.

And something else was starting to happen. The green lights flickered on and off crazily, then a bright red one, and then pitch black—nothing, like the blank screen. A whistle screeched, so high and loud Di thought it was exploding from inside her head.

She heard someone scream, "It's grinding down—get out!!"

A metallic heaving came from below, sparks streamed up through the floor grating all around them: now chugging from below, a fury in the great howling generators below, sputtering, and the floor grating was bouncing up under their feet. Folsom Energy was shuddering to a full stop.

Di, Oki, and Ham were now loose, and Thea stepped out from behind one of the big cylinders. Tom leaped down, and had the lead and moved in a wild zigzag. At least one security guard, maybe two, were closing in from behind. The metal floor was clanging, ripping, splitting open in places like an old fishing net; it was like the earth was about to spit out its core. Tom turned his hat backward and flew, the others behind him—toward the tunnels.

LOCKDOWN

THEY HIT THE TUNNEL ENTRANCE AT FULL SPEED, whipping past every bulge and cranny. If they could make it out of the x-pipe they still had a chance to get away. Piling out into the open x-pipe, blinking in the bright light, Tom in front, the group landed, with Tom now loping toward the pipe mouth. The sun was up, and the glare nearly blinded them as they ran. The pipe seemed to shrink, crowded with dark silhouettes, some real, others shadows.

Its walls were trembling, as if the whole island was about to blow. Tom slowed a step as he neared the opening. He hooked his fingers into a crack along the pipe mouth and swung out like a chimpanzee to catch the lip of the rock shelf. But something hit him in midair and threw him backward into Oki, who tumbled back into Di, they went down like dominoes, and Di could see Tom kind of bounce, and tumble—back out!

"What the—!" someone screamed, and Di dove back toward the pipe mouth for Tom's tiny hands, now dug into the bottom of the pipe mouth, slipping, his body dangling outside.

She almost had one of his hands when another blast—it was wind, air—lifted Tom up and spun him right back into the pipe again, whipping his Angels hat off and back down the pipe.

"Ham! Help me, someone!"

And suddenly the sun was gone—blocked—and Di glanced up and saw what it was. The helicopter, the same one from early in the morning. Black and shiny, its side door open, two commando guys crouching there, like out of the movies.

Lockdown.

"Holy mama, that clown's got a freakin' gun on us!" Ham yelled.

Di, half seated, backpedaled with all her might—she had Tom's hands now—and Thea yanked them back in. And then everything slowed down. Ham danced forward and heaved a huge stone and it clattered hard off the windshield of the copter. Di saw it so clearly, that heavy thing bouncing off the screen, that she knew it was not a stone but a piece of the pipe. A plate-size piece she had seen herself. A row of thumping little puffs ran up the floor of the pipe like a zipper, dust spraying everywhere.

“Are they shooting? Are they shooting at kids!” Ham yelled.

The light exploded back through the mouth; the thumping black ship had moved away.

Di stared for long enough to see a rope with a grappling hook clang up into the pipe and yelled, “Ruuun!” and sneakers squeaked and she saw someone’s keypad drop and Tom’s hat was on the ground, and wild-eyed with adrenaline she fled with the others and darted into the tunnel back toward the y-pipe.

Di scooped up the Angels hat and jammed it into her back pocket on the way in. No chance security would get them now, Di thought, not from behind anyway. Adults were too big to move quickly through here and probably couldn’t fit at all down and through the puddle on the other side.

If anyone made it that far. Now the danger was in front of them: the water cannon. She had lost all sense of time and had no idea if it was still running.

It was. The watery thunder sounded as soon as they were about halfway through the tunnel, and as they got closer they could feel some spray. Closer still the water ricocheted through the tunnel and filled it up to their knees, before draining away. The old tunnel doors were worthless, Di thought.

This mess of a plant was rotting out the entire island the whole time they lived up there, oblivious.

Tom, in the lead, stopped when the water was coming up

to about their ankles. Di saw from the way he was moving that he was loopy, almost silly, reckless; he must have been so surprised he was alive, just as she had been after going over the cliff, that he didn't care anymore. He had been timing the blasts coming through the y-pipe, timing them for weeks. He knew the rhythm, but no one had any idea if it would be the same now, with the plant shutting down.

Tom didn't seem to notice or care. "From here," he shouted, "you got about seven seconds to make it into the pipe and over to the other side, before the next blast. Enough for two people to go at a time."

"It better be," someone else screamed.

Tom went first. Ham trailed him and stopped at the y-pipe, and watched to make sure he got across. In the rumbling darkness Di had no idea what happened. She prayed to herself. Let him make it. Let something good happen, please.

Ham finally came back to the group. He signaled a thumbs up. "He's through," he said. The whole episode seemed to take forever, Di thought. It seemed to her that the water level where they were was rising each time the pipe blasted. Her shoulders ached and she was dizzy for a moment: She was sure the walls were closing on them. She was doing all she could not to start screaming madly.

Ham waited for the next break, grabbed Oki's hand, and Di

saw them go and couldn't help herself from lunging to follow them. Thea held her back.

"Why now?" Di screamed. "Why do we have to split up everybody now?" But no one heard her. She held her head and rubbed her temples and the endless rumble-crash of the water made her suddenly cold, and shivering, out of control.

The sound died off, and now she was moving. She and Thea. Plowing head down through the draining warm water, using Thea's hand to pull herself forward, head down and moving just because there was nothing else to do.

And here was the pipe—gleaming, slippery—and she was down on the floor, Thea too, and Di heard herself cry out something about the time, the seconds. Why couldn't they get out of here—why? Her legs loose and heavy as thick noodles, the rumble starting in the throat of the great pipe, and then she saw Thea climb into the tunnel and reach back her big hand—and Di glimpsed a flash of red behind her.

The Angels hat. On the pipe floor.

She didn't think about it. It was instinct. It was the hat. She reached back to scoop it up and in that second the freight train of water went through her as if she wasn't there. Thea had her hand one moment, and the next she was gone.

Princess Di saw a wall of white, and no breath, and then all went black.

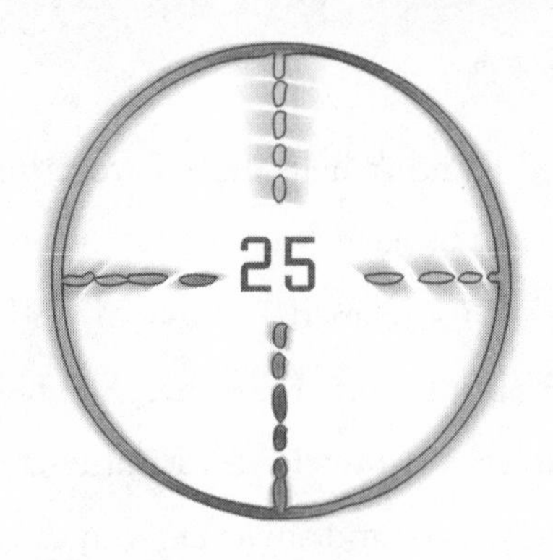

THIS BLUE HEAVEN

SHE CARTWHEELED FROM THE OPENING OF THE FOUR- slope and down, down, a 30-degree angle at least. She had wondered about this right triangle before and put it out of her mind, afraid to imagine the reality.

As she raced through the chute, the map took over her mind: 40 yards on the cliff side, and another 70 yards from the lip of the cliff back to where the pipe started to angle down. That made the distance the square root of [(40 × 40) + (70 × 70)]. About 80 yards, give or take, she had once calculated. Nearly the length of a football field. And the force of that water blast behind you.

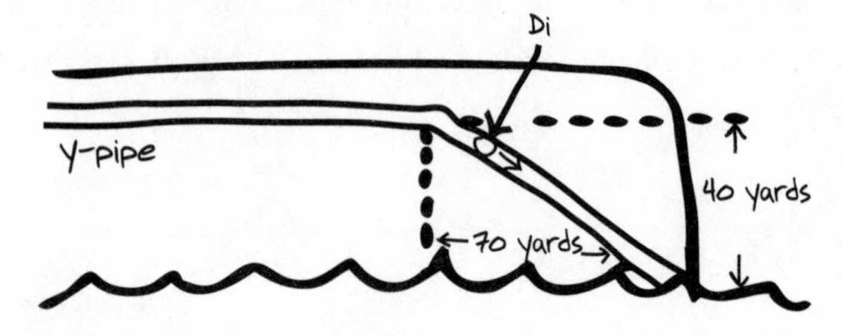

How fast would you go? How deep into that pool at the bottom of the cove would you shoot? Would you hit the bottom? Would you even be alive?

Flickers of blue and black blotted out the map, and for a while she thought that she might be entering heaven. An end to the foul tunnels at last. A terrible crash. No breath. Floating worm-like things in front of her eyes: Did heaven have those?

All at once her head broke through thick glass into an empty world of shimmering light—sunlight?—and she blinked and vomited and her lungs gurgled. Burned. Death could not be this painful, could it? Being dead?

She suddenly saw the island from a distance and imagined for a moment she might be a ghost, floating away. She was too wet for that: She was in the water, floating out to the open sea. Something dark came from behind, and she turned to see a wall of green-gray water. She tried weakly to duck under it but the great rolling weight of the wave lifted her high and pushed her down, down, spinning again, so deep her ears popped—and nothing here but the green-blue empty deep.

Again her head broke through the surface and into the open sunlight, and she closed her eyes and vomited again and waited for the story to end. All of it.

She would not survive another wave, and when she felt

some tentacle wrap around her waist, she went limp. The arm seemed to lift her up. An octopus maybe? She didn't care. She pried her eyes open for one last look but saw only a small window of light in front of her—as if looking through another tunnel—and then even that snapped shut. Nothing.

THE RETURN

THE BLAST OF WATER HAD KNOCKED THEA A FEW FEET back into the four-slope tunnel. She stumbled forward, and fell to her knees in front of Ham and the others, screaming.

"She went back!" Thea was yelling and crying at the same time. "She turned and went back! She went back in!"

Tom looked stricken, like he'd seen a ghost. Like his mind was capsizing again; he doubled over in pain, rubbing his stomach to stop it from hurting.

Ham took his shoulder. "Look. It's water. Water. It's getting close to high tide—she would have landed in that cove down there."

He looked around at the others.

"Stop, everybody. Stop!" he yelled between water blasts. "We have to get out of here and go see if we can find her. We know where she has to be, but can we stop crying about it and maybe try to find her?" Thea was nodding and tried to dry her face on her soaked shirt. Tom was trying to stand. Oki was making a low moaning sound.

Ham got them out of the tunnel. With the Trashmore exit blocked, they would have to climb out of the negative side of the x-axis pipe. The cliffs were steeper on the other side, Thea told them; it should be OK.

No one seemed to hear. Barely able to walk, ears ringing from the water blasts, numb now, they only wanted out. They rested near the mouth for a few minutes, avoiding each other's eyes, staring down or out over the ocean. Thea stuck her head out of the pipe and checked the surrounding rock for footholds. She stared for a while, nodded, and then motioned for them to follow. An electric crackling sound stopped them. A radio sound—Oki's radio, the one Hog had given him. A miracle it still worked. Loud static and it crackled again.

"Sonny? Oki? Where are you, pick the thing up, willya?"

Oki pressed the button. "Pop, I'm here. I'm here!"

The sound of a familiar voice from the land brought life back into his face. The others felt it too—Adjacent people knew they were underground.

"Thanks be to all," the voice barked. "It's about time you picked up. Now listen to me. I don't know what's happening down there but there are helicopters buzzing all over up here.

Police and government and I don't know what. I just heard on the scanner that the Crotona police are coming over here in force."

A hushing static rolled through the box. Then he was back. "You hear that? I think the Croutons are even coming out to rescue us. You did it. Now get your bones back up here."

"Coming," Oki yelled into the radio. "Coming, Pop!"

Once out of the pipe, Thea took the lead, climbing out of the opening, then winding up toward the top.

Arms and legs throbbing with pain, their vision blurring. Exhausted. The climb was steep, and Ham dropped back behind the younger boys. Those two looked like they could fall at any moment. The top was just up ahead and Thea turned and gave a thumbs-up when the sky blackened. Pounding gusts hit them in the back.

Thea turned and screamed as crazy as old Blue Moon.

Tom and Oki hugged the rock with all the strength they had left. Ham didn't even turn to look. He knew the helicopter had circled to find them, and this time there was no cover. Perched on a small ledge, he swung his arms and yelled at them like a madman and then turned his back. Then unbuckled his belt and dropped his pants.

"Here's a target, you twisted clowns!" he screamed, bending over and wagging his butt. "Hit this with a satellite missile."

But they didn't shoot. The helicopter hovered there, as if

trying to decide what to do, and after a few seconds banked and peeled away, over the water.

"What just happened?" Thea yelled. "Did he do what I think he did?"

No one had the energy to answer, not even Ham. The climbers, now stiff and shivering cold, continued hand over raw hand. Thea helped them up and over the edge of the island.

There they collapsed. Lay in the sun, eyes closed, breathing. Breathing the open air of the living world. Tom got them up.

"Diaphanta," he said. "Lady Di. We have to go." They straggled in toward Adjacent like refugees from a shipwreck, bruised, soaked, and filthy. A crowd had gathered out on the road, and when the four came into sight their parents ran out to them. Mr. Muhammad and Mrs. Smith; Mr. and Mrs. Hutchison—Thea's parents—and Mr. Rowan and Hog.

Tom fell into his father's arms and whispered urgently in the man's ear: "Di. Lady Di. The Point. She went in."

Mr. Muhammad was busy spinning his son around in his arms and at first had no idea what the boy was saying. He thought Tom was rambling, delusional. "Calm down, boy," he said. "It's just your mind, let it go."

Tom got more desperate, and when his father looked up to see Mrs. Smith circling frantically, hysterical, he understood.

"Where exactly?" he said, holding Tom in front of him by the shoulders. "Tell me where!"

Tom Jones led the way. Tom holding his father's hand and giving directions, dozens of others following now, murmuring and subdued. Thea carried Oki, and Ham scraped along in his shredded clothes and hair so matted and dirty it was forming dreadlocks.

Hog pulled up the rear, along with Ham's dad, who waddled like a walrus. On the way through Adjacent there were signs of life returning. Crotona police cars, two of them, doors open; old pickups full of furniture; radios blaring. Two Folsom security guards handcuffed together in their Jeep.

Everyone seemed to stop what they were doing when Tom and his crew passed by. The only helicopter in sight was a small news chopper, high overhead. By the time they reached the Point, Tom had his hands over his eyes. He didn't want to see Mrs. Clarke's empty trailer, or their old meeting place. Most of all he didn't want to see what might be down in the cove. Or what might not be there. An empty horizon, no sign of anything. The wide swallowing sea.

He asked his dad to put him down before they reached the cliff's edge. He sat there, with his back to the water, his hands over his eyes. His father stood by him, anxious, uncertain.

Thea and Ham approached to comfort him but they saw the look on his face and moved past. Even after all they'd done together, they had no idea what to make of Tom Jones. Ham was beginning to think the quiet, small boy was more of a lunatic than he himself was. Thea was the one who moved to the front of the group and raised her voice.

"Hey, everybody! Could everyone just stay back for a minute here, while I go down and look? We don't know what happened to Lady Di, and maybe the parents will want to wait before letting the younger kids look."

Wait they did, quiet now, unsure of how to feel or what to say. The sea roared below, and a cold winter wind swept down from the hills behind Crotona. Thea rounded the fence by the Point, and found the trailhead.

By now the crowd had swelled behind her, everyone staring as if watching some burning car wreck with the people still trapped inside. Thea climbed down a short distance and stopped. Her head was still visible just above the ground, jaw slack.

Then a kind of silent gasp went through the crowd, with Thea's head just floating there, like she'd seen a ghost. She was staring, her hand to her mouth. She turned and ran back up the slope.

"What kind of twisted show is this—" someone began.

Someone else screamed.

Big and ugly as a sea creature came Blue Moon with his beat-up surfboard under one arm and Lady Di over the other shoulder. Those silver snakes of hair coiling over his back, mingling with thin strands of orange. Black and shiny as an eel in his wetsuit, he seemed to be rising out of the center of the earth.

Typical Moon, he didn't say a word or even nod hello. To anyone. He just walked through the crowd like a barefoot Paul Bunyan and over the dusty gravel all the way to Mrs. Clarke's place. Stopped, leaned over, and gently placed Di down on one of the plastic patio chairs.

She nearly capsized in the chair, making a kind of bubbling gurgling sound. Alive. It was Ham who grabbed Tom, walked the hunched boy over, and sat him down next to her. Mrs. Smith of course ran up and fell to her knees and hugged Di, lost her mind in the way that parents can. Then she kind of hugged them both together—she was like that—and Tom fell off his plastic chair. He looked so different now. No hat, and people saw his face probably for the first time.

The pair sat there for a long time, Di and Tom, on the very spot where the insanity had started. A lifetime ago, it seemed.

Mrs. Smith brought over some blankets. Muhammad and Rene D. brought food, kebabs and tortillas and sauces. Mrs. Polya came by with a case of diet cream soda. Mr. Paulos from DeepEnd Liquors was there too. He brought some homemade beer. Terrible stuff. Even Ham's dad wouldn't touch it.

After a while lots of people wandered off, to finish moving back in or to start dinner. The main group stayed, though. The tunnel crawlers and their parents and friends. Stayed and ate and talked a little.

It was all kind of hard to describe, even if you were standing right there watching. The smell of the ocean stung your nose, and that cold and dead-clear sky looked like some giant blood orange, when the sun poured off into the ocean. Adjacent could be like that sometimes, dead lame as it was.

On the way back, Tom, who had not said a word the whole time, finally asked Di what she was going to do tomorrow. Sleep, she said. Sleep.

"Maybe I'll come by later, though," she said. "We can maybe do, you know, nothing."

MALBA CLARKE

HERE'S THE THING, AND ANYONE CAN TELL YOU. PEOPLE told that helicopter story about a billion times. Sure, they would mention the tunnels, the plant, the clues; and maybe riff on Pythagoras, pi, Cartesian coordinates, and all. If they were really good, they'd even spin out some mind-bending problem, like, say, how to estimate pi using the Pythagorean theorem. But it was all just a buildup to, "Then Ham, I swear to you, Ham shot a red-eye at that sucker and drove the twisted pigs away!"

And it never, ever got old.

For the rest, well, you could read it in the newspapers if you really wanted to know. The federal government did come in and close Folsom for a while, after arresting executives who were going to stage an accident in order to shut down Adjacent and stash plant waste product under the empty trailers. Totally, seriously illegal. They arrested the security man and Mr. Pink (their huge faces were in the paper). They found our Adjacent locals, Mr. Romo and Mrs. Quartez, who spent time in a hospital and are back now. Mrs. Clarke, well, it was the strangest thing. They found her with the others, locked up in the plant. But they took the old lady to Washington, D.C., of all places, for "debriefing" at a military or CIA hospital, whatever that is. The article called Mrs. Clarke a "former math teacher who brought down a major conspiracy by leaving math clues." They said she would be given some kind of medal by the government.

She did write, though, which was something. The letter was addressed to Di and Tom and arrived at Di's, with a stamp and everything. It was short, and a few of us got to read it.

Here's what it said:

> I hardly know what to say except thank you both. Thank you for trying to find me, even though you had no idea where to start. For not giving up, even though I know you were afraid to fail every step of the way. I am sorry about some of the clues, how vague they were. I placed them there in a hurry, when I suspected I might be in danger.
>
> I am sorry for something else too—that there was no one reliable to guide you,

to advise you, even to let you know you were on the right track. That will change, I promise. Trying to solve a hard problem: that is everything, and people will see it written on your faces. Your effort by itself will draw others to you. I imagine it has already happened.

Most of all, though, I thank you for working so hard even though I know you thought that it would make no difference at all—not to me, to you, or to anyone else. It has and it will.

Then she wrote, "All my love," and signed off with just an "M" followed by a simple equation: 4 - 3 = 7, followed by a string of other meaningless-looking symbols. That was probably a joke, but no one could say for sure.

Well, no one except for maybe Di and Tom. But you'd have to ask them.

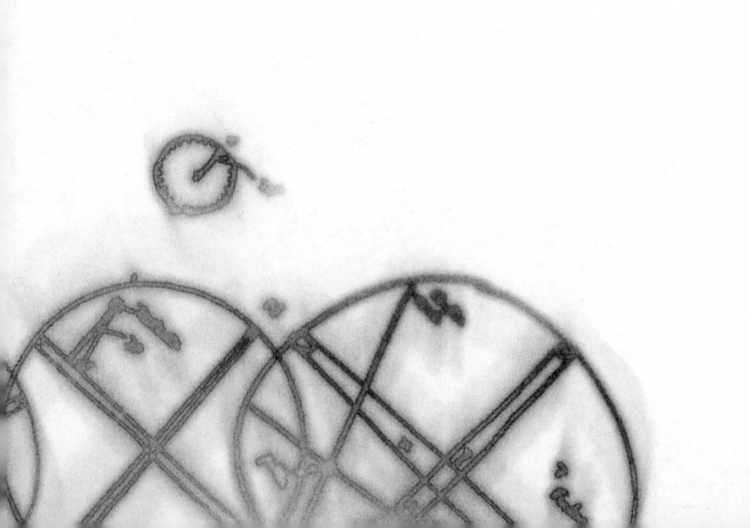

ABOUT THE AUTHOR

BENEDICT CAREY

is a reporter who has written about medicine and science for magazines and newspapers. He graduated from a large Midwestern university with a degree in math, and within months had forgotten almost all of it. He now works as a science reporter for the *New York Times.*

THIS BOOK WAS ART DIRECTED

and designed by Chad W. Beckerman. The text is set in 12-point Adobe Garamond, a typeface based on those created in the sixteenth century by Claude Garamond. Garamond modeled his typefaces on ones created by Venetian printers at the end of the fifteenth century. The modern version used in this book was designed by Robert Slimbach, who studied Garamond's historic typefaces at the Plantin-Moretus Museum in Antwerp, Belgium. The interior illustrations were created with Adobe Illustrator CS3.

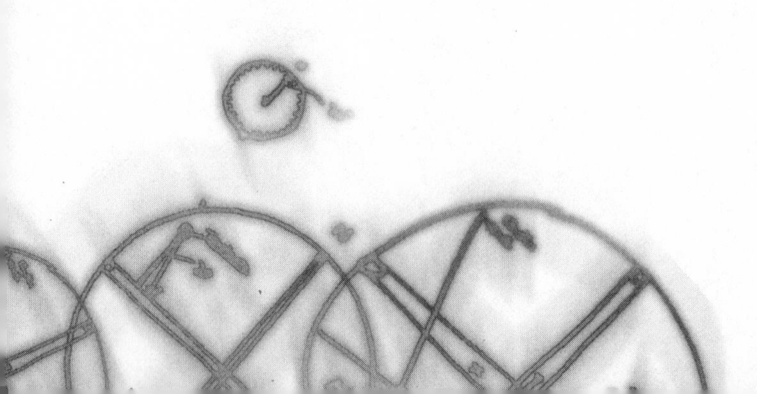